Behind the Mountains

first

person

fiction

Behind

SCHOLASTIC INC.

New York   Toronto   London   Auckland   Sydney
Mexico City   New Delhi   Hong Kong   Buenos Aires

the Mountains

Edwidge Danticat

ISBN 0-439-53112-8

12 11 10 9 8 7 6 5 4 3 2 1   3 4 5 6 7 8/0

Printed in the U.S.A.   23

First Scholastic Paper-Over-Board printing, March 2003

For Nadira and Ezekiel Danticat

Beau Jour, Haiti

Wednesday, October 18, 2000

Ti liv mwen, my sweet little book. How wonderful to have your crisp white pages to write on during those quiet moments between my day and afternoon tasks. My teacher, Madame Auguste, gave you to me today before we started recitations. In front of the entire class, she said I deserved you because I had the best marks of all thirty-nine pupils last month. Madame Auguste is like that. Every now and then she will surprise the class with a kind gesture, such as a group outing or candies from the city, but this time she just chose me. She gave you to me.

It was Madame Auguste's opinion that I could use you in whatever way I wanted, keep you in the little cedar box you came in and never take you out at all, or only remove you from there on special occasions. She also said that I could keep you in a special place at home. For me that would be under my pillow on the bed that Manman and I sleep in together.

"Celiane could also use her notebook," she said,

spelling out every word for the students to ponder, "to write down *pensées* or maxims that she likes so she can refer to them whenever it pleases her. She may use this book to jot down the pages of the texts she has to memorize for recitations in class, or she can simply use it to record her own ideas, thoughts of her own."

Madame Auguste made such a speech of the whole thing to show me and the other pupils all the uses an empty notebook can have. But when she said I could use you to write down things about myself, I became very glad and decided that is exactly what I am going to do. I will tell you everything I can tell no one else, and you will keep quiet because you have no tongue and you cannot speak. My pen is your tongue and I am your voice so you will never betray my secrets.

I must go soon, sweet little book, to prepare for Manman's return from the market. Manman goes to the market down the mountain in Léogâne on Wednesdays and Saturdays to sell peanut and coconut confections that she, my older brother, Moy, and I make together. Manman will be back soon, at just about the time that Moy will be returning from the cornfields. Ever since Papa left for New York five years ago, it is Moy who looks after Papa's cornfields and Papa's two pride cows.

I must do my homework before Manman and Moy return. Then I must go to the fork in the road and help Manman carry the provisions she has brought home from the market. I wish I had gotten you sooner, sweet little book. But as Manman always says, you cannot chew before you have teeth. Maybe Madame Auguste was waiting for me to know how to use you before giving you to me. I will "chew on you" later.

Later

I am writing behind our house, by the light of our kerosene lamp. Manman and Moy are asleep. I sneaked out to the cooking shed where the three large rocks we use to hold our pots are still warm from the fire Moy had made for Manman to prepare our supper. In spite of Moy having poured half a calabash of water on the cooking sticks, there are a few cinders left in the ashes, small pieces of wood glowing red before collapsing into a heap of white soot.

I love to watch the ashes, especially at night. It's

like finding stars on the ground, an extraordinary thing to observe in an ordinary place, the place where we cook our food.

Our house is not big, but we are very proud of it because my father built it himself many years ago. Papa was proud of this house, too, when he was here. He told everyone who made a compliment about the house, "I built it with my two hands."

Papa had refused help from his neighbors and friends because he wanted to prove to Manman's parents — Granmè Melina and Granpè Nozial — that he was worthy of her. This is why we have stayed here in this same house since Papa left even though he sends us money from New York and we could afford a place in the city, like Papa's sister, Tante Rose.

Our house has two rooms. The front room is for us to receive guests. It's also where Moy sleeps. The back room is for Manman and Papa, but now I sleep with Manman in her and Papa's bed. (When Papa was here, I slept on a sisal mat on the floor next to the bed.)

Our house is in a village called Beau Jour. It is a tiny village on top of a mountain. Beau Jour is on the middle mountain of a range of four mountains that we can see in every direction. I learned from my geography lesson that the name of this country, Haiti, comes from the Arawak Indian word *Ayiti*, which means mountainous land or land on high.

There is also a proverb that says, "Behind the mountains are more mountains." This is certainly true because our house is on a mountain, but not the tallest one. Some mountains are bigger and taller still.

From our house, when it is not so dark like it is tonight, I can see a chain of mountains and braids of water running down the mountains to become water-falls and rivers. In the daytime, when the sun is high in the sky, you almost cannot see the water at all, just a glow mixed in with the sun. It looks like the pictures of crystals and diamonds in the books Madame Auguste keeps in the schoolhouse. The mountains are more beautiful still at sunset. Then they look blue and gold, like one of the paintings that Moy's artist friend, Bòs Dezi, makes to sell at the tourist market in the capital, Port-au-Prince.

I must admit that I am afraid of the dark, even though you would not know it because I am out here alone so late at night. My grandfather, Granpè Nozial, sometimes tells very scary stories about the night. One of the scariest stories is about a three-legged horse named Galipòt, who trots down the mountains at night looking for his fourth leg. The three-legged horse is named Galipòt because if you say the three syllables really fast "Ga-li-pòt-Ga-li-pòt-Ga-li-pòt," it makes the sound of three hooves hitting the ground. If you see Galipòt and run, he thinks you're his fourth leg and he chases you.

I have never seen this horse myself, and most of the time I believe, as Papa used to say, that maybe these kinds of things only exist in the "streams of our dreams."

Thursday, October 19

Last night I did not share the biggest news. Manman came home with a cassette from Papa. After supper, the three of us gathered in the front room to listen to the cassette.

Papa sends us cassettes and money from New York once a month. Papa sends the money to pay for my schooling and for Moy's training to be a tailor. (Moy chose that himself rather than going to university in the city.) Moy uses a lot of his money to buy sketching paper. Even though Manman thinks he is making de-

6

signs for shirts and pants for his tailor's classes, I have looked over his shoulder a few times and I have seen that he is really drawing shapes and faces like Bòs Dezi does before he makes one of his paintings. Sometimes Moy draws girls, too, but never anyone I know.

The money Papa sends us also pays for food and clothes, and any extra things we need. Manman does not really have to sell *dous* at the market, but with Papa gone, she likes to keep herself busy and she likes for us to keep ourselves occupied, too. So she works at making and selling the confections and Moy works the cornfields and looks after Papa's cows even when Moy also has to go to tailor school.

Sometimes Moy comes home angry because his classmates tease him and say, "Your papa is in New York. Why must you work the fields?" Moy has gotten into fights because of this. Just last week he punched a classmate, who then hit Moy on the shoulder with a stick. I don't know all the details. That's all Moy was willing to say about it.

Manman is worried that Moy is becoming too difficult. She blames his behavior on the fact that Papa is gone. I don't think she is blaming Papa, just his absence. Whenever Moy gets into one of his fights, Manman always makes it clear to him that she is the *granmoun*, the adult, and that he is the child — Moy is nineteen and not a child, but to Manman he will always be one. You should see Manman standing on her toes to make herself the same height as Moy to scold him.

"Listen to me, Moy, the head that's accustomed to wearing a hat will always wear a hat," she says to him.

I wasn't sure what she was trying to tell Moy then, but now I realize that maybe she was telling him that if he gets used to being in fights, he would always be fighting.

Manman likes to speak in pictures like that. They are called proverbs. I like proverbs because you have to stop and think to interpret them. They make a picture for you and you must discover for yourself how to interpret it.

In any case, after supper we all sit in the front room with the cassette machine that Papa had bought for us before he left for New York. Manman brought new batteries from the market, which she puts in the machine before inserting the cassette.

Papa always begins his cassettes to us in the same way.

"Alo, Aline." (That's Manman.)

Then it's, "Alo, Moy, alo, Celiane."

Papa continues, "How are you, my precious ones? I am trying to see all three of you in my mind as I sit here. Aline, I see your face leaning close to the machine as if you would like to touch my voice. Celiane, I see you pulling at a little strand of hair on the left side of your face because you are waiting for Papa to say your name."

Papa knows us well. It is true Manman was leaning forward as though she wanted to kiss Papa's voice and I was doing the same, except I was also pulling on my hair. Moy was leaning back in his chair, just as Papa said. He was trying to appear calm and unexcited. (I wonder if Manman tells Papa in secret that this is what we do while listening to his cassettes.)

Each month when Papa sends the cassettes, I worry that he will forget to mention my name, or forget to talk about the few things I had said to him in the last cassette we had all made for him together.

"Moy, I hope your lessons are going well," Papa says.

Moy smiles, losing some of his reserve.

Papa tells Moy, "Manman says you are still taking time to look after the land the way Papa taught you. This makes Papa proud. You might not think it fashionable, but, Moy, everything you do now will be valuable to you in the future."

Most of the time when Papa is talking in the cassettes, I think he forgets himself, forgets that he is talking to us and simply talks to himself, to console himself, to counsel himself just as he is counseling us, to make himself feel better just as he is trying to make us feel better.

It was my turn for Papa to speak to me.

"Celiane, Papa is glad that you got such good marks in school last month," he says. "Papa will reward you by sending you a typewriter like you asked."

I scream so loud that some birds stir in the almond trees in the yard; I scare them away with my voice.

Now comes the moment both Moy and I were expecting. This moment comes in all the cassettes.

"Aline," Papa says, "after these words you can stop the cassette. The rest is for your ears alone."

"Good-bye, Moy. Good-bye, Cécé," Papa says before

he speaks to Manman alone. "You are in all of Papa's dreams and you have all of Papa's love."

Manman turns off the cassette. The rest she listens to when Moy and I are away from the house. She listens to the cassettes almost every day, until the next one comes or until the batteries die.

Manman always looks sad when it is time to stop listening to the part of the cassette that we all listen to together. It is as if Papa was with all of us for a while and has disappeared again. I know she feels better, though, once she listens to her part alone. Papa says things to her, good news and bad, that he chooses not to share with Moy and me.

Friday, October 20

My closest friend in school is a girl named Thérèse. Thérèse and I are together so much that some of the other pupils think we are sisters. We are both tall for our age, taller than all of the boys, especially a boy named Pouchon, who is always mad at me because I am usually first in the class, while he is in second place behind me.

I am flattered to be mistaken for Thérèse's sister because she is pretty. Everyone, even Pouchon, thinks so. What is different about us, though, is that Thérèse is not nearly as interested in school as I am. All she thinks about are boys, not the ones in our class, but older boys, like my brother, Moy, who is her latest fancy.

Thérèse lives in the same village as my grandparents. Whenever Manman, Moy, and I go to my grandparents' house, we must pass her house, and whenever she knows we are coming, she stands out on the road in front of her house to greet us. (Mostly to greet Moy.)

Today during recess Thérèse started pestering me again about Moy. Some of my classmates were playing hopscotch, marbles, jumping rope, and singing while they twirled themselves to near dizziness in a *won*, but all Thérèse wanted to do was talk about Moy.

"How is your brother, Celiane?"

"He is fine, Thérèse."

"Is he still going to Léogâne for sewing lessons?"

"They are not sewing lessons. He is learning to be a tailor."

"Then one day I will be a tailor's wife."

"You're dreaming, Thérèse."

"Okay, Celiane, for now you can keep your brother to yourself, but soon I will be looking for someone and I will be sure he looks at me."

"He has seen you already, Thérèse."

"He has seen me with his eyes closed, Celiane. Soon he will look at me with his eyes open."

I would never tell Thérèse about the girls in Moy's sketches. If she knew about them she would die of jealousy.

Later

This afternoon we made the *dous* for Manman to sell at the market tomorrow. First, we boiled the milk from our cows with the sugar that Manman bought at the market, and then we put in the peanuts and coconut chunks. It is my job to shell the peanuts and Moy's to shred the coconut.

While the *dous* was cooling off, we made a cassette for Papa. We sat together and took turns talking to him.

Manman usually speaks first.

"Victor," she says, "we, your family, are happy to have this chance to talk to you again. We welcomed with great joy the words you sent us last month. Now I will let the children greet you."

Moy leans over to speak. He begins by clearing his throat. "Papa, thank you for the money you continue to send for my schooling. I am progressing well. The corn is coming along fine. The cows are okay. I will speak to you again next month."

After I say a few things to Papa, Manman takes the cassette machine to her room.

Unlike Papa who was alone when he spoke in the cassettes, we were all together in one room, which made us very shy, except for Manman who would later say private words to Papa while we were asleep.

There is so much I always plan to tell Papa, but I am always embarrassed to talk in front of Manman and Moy. I am better at writing, so maybe I should write him letters. I have written a letter for one other person, so why not for Papa?

Once, when I was at the market in Léogâne with Manman, one of the cloth vendors, a lady named Sò Grace, waited until Manman was gone on one of her errands and asked if I could read a letter for her. She reaches into her money apron and hands me the letter. It is from her daughter in Canada.

I read the letter to her, translating it from the French into Creole. Then Sò Grace asks me if I can write a reply to her daughter.

The daughter was studying at a university in Québec and was writing to tell her mother that she was doing well in her studies and that she had met a young man whom she wanted to marry. Sò Grace beams when I read and interpret this for her. At the same time she seems so sorrowful that she has been carrying such good news in her money apron and has not been able to read it.

She gives me five dollars to buy paper and an envelope to write a reply to her daughter. The rest I am allowed to keep for myself.

She tells me to write to her daughter how happy she is that her daughter is almost an engineer, and to ask if she is sure about the young man. Is it the right time to marry? Will the marriage not distract her from her studies, halt the beginning of her career?

I write exactly what she says, pretending that she is giving me dictation, like Madame Auguste in class.

I am careful with my handwriting, and the letter comes out neat with no mistakes.

Now I think I will do the same for Papa. I will write him letters that only he can read.

I quickly began my letter. I planned to tell him so much that I was too shy to tell him in front of the others.

Dear Papa,
We miss you.
Your daughter Celiane

I was surprised so little came out in my letter. Maybe I don't know my own father anymore. Maybe he has changed. Maybe I have changed.

Even though Papa sends us pictures regularly, it is hard to imagine what he looks like in his everyday life, in the place where he works, in the house where he lives. I am even more worried now that I will not know what to say to Papa when I see him again.

Saturday, October 21

We wake before dawn to go to the market. At that time of the morning, a gray mist hangs in the air, dew over everything. It is very calm but a little cool at the

16

same time. Manman makes me wear an extra blouse over my dress. Halfway down the mountain, when the sun comes up, I can take off the blouse.

My job is to carry the peanut confections while Manman carries the coconut ones.

Along the way we meet other vendors walking down to the market. Some are carrying plantains, breadfruits, mangoes, and corn to sell. Others are carrying cocoa and coffee beans.

We must cross a river before we can reach the market. Manman and the other vendors always try and find the shallowest spot in the river for their crossing. Then we remove our shoes, raise our skirts — the men roll up their pants — and we wade across with baskets of different weights on top of our heads.

The market is very lively on Saturdays, even more so than on Wednesdays. Manman does not have a stall, because she is not a big vendor like Sò Grace or the others who sell things in larger quantities. Manman usually sets her winnowing trays near Sò Grace's stall, and Sò Grace doesn't mind if Manman benefits from the shade from her stall because Manman buys cloth from her now and then.

Sò Grace is taking out some of her best cloth when

we arrive. Soon Manman goes off to send the cassette to Papa. I have decided not to send my letter until I can think of more to say.

While Manman is gone, Sò Grace walks over to where I am sitting behind Manman's tray of sweets and says, "My daughter is coming for a visit soon."

"Is she, Madame?" I say.

Sò Grace bends down, picks up one of Manman's coconut candies, and bites into it. Then she reaches into her money apron and gives me twenty-five *gourdes*, which is much more than the *dous* is worth.

"When I spoke to her on the telephone," she says, "my daughter told me your letter was the best letter that I'd ever had written for me. She said she could hear my voice in the letter."

Later

Moy met us at the fork in the road when we returned from the market. Manman was more tired than usual. She had a headache.

Moy gave me a gentle tap on the head as a greeting, like he always does. When you look at him, not thinking that he is your brother, Moy does appear rather handsome. He is tall and thin, like Papa, and he wears loose and airy clothes that he makes himself.

Even though he and Manman are not on the best of terms, Moy takes Manman's basket and carries it the rest of the way home.

Sunday, October 22

We are at Granmè Melina and Granpè Nozial's house for Sunday supper. Granmè Melina made my favorite dish, green peas with rice.

Granmè Melina is young for a grandmother. Both she and Granpè Nozial have strong, firm bodies. They still work their own fields. They do not live with Manman because they say it would make them age faster having someone looking after them.

Behind Granmè Melina and Granpè Nozial's house are the graves of Granmè Melina's parents. Every year on the Day of the Dead, Granmè Melina cleans the graves to honor her parents.

While I am washing the pots in the yard, even though I am not trying to listen, I hear Granpè Nozial and Manman talking about Moy.

"You cannot keep him under your skirt for the rest

of his life," Granpè Nozial tells Manman. "He is a young man, Aline. Young men are like young bulls. They must fight their way through everything."

Monday, October 23

I keep thinking about Papa. When he was here, some nights after working in the fields, he would stand in the yard with Moy and me, and together we would look up at the sky and watch the stars fall. Though he would not speak, Papa would look sad when a star fell out of the sky. It was as though the world was changed somehow, and not for the better.

Things were sometimes very bad for Papa, like when his crops failed and he had to sell some of his land to repay his debts. He was too proud to ask his younger sister, Tante Rose, for money.

Papa finally left for New York because he was worried that one year things would become too difficult to bear: A cyclone or hurricane would hit, or the crops would fail and we would have nothing at all.

It was a childhood friend of Papa's, Franck, who sent him the invitation papers. Franck has several restaurants in New York and offered Papa at one of them. Papa was supposed to go for only a few months, but then he stayed.

Three years ago, Papa's friend Franck sent invitation papers to the American consulate for Manman, Moy, and me. We have already had all of our physical examinations and as soon as we receive word from the consulate, we will be able to join Papa in New York.

Tuesday, October 24

Tonight we had a rain shower. Thérèse and I were doing homework together when the rain began. When I was younger, I used to be afraid of lightning and thunder so I would hide under a sheet during rain showers.

When Papa was here, he and Moy would soap themselves then rush out in the rain in their underpants. Thérèse and I wanted to go out for a rain bath, but Manman would not let us.

Moy went out rain bathing, but hurried back inside saying the rain was too cold. There were bits of hail the size of rice grains in it.

Thérèse was so happy to see Moy in his underpants that she laughed and laughed, her laughter sounding even louder than the rain pounding on the tin roof.

I love to hear Thérèse laugh. It is a very free laugh. Thérèse never covers her mouth when she laughs. She just lets it out with all her might. Her whole body bounces. Her neck twists. Her chest rattles. Her hands wave wildly in the air, as though they were dancing.

Manman says that Thérèse laughs like someone who was raised with pigs and donkeys. I believe Thérèse laughs like someone who thinks she may never laugh again.

Wednesday, October 25

Manman was very tired today when she came home from the market. This happens to her sometimes. She gets so fatigued that her bones ache. Her head still aches, too.

Before she went to bed, I made her some ginger tea and Moy boiled a yam for her. I could tell she didn't have much of an appetite, but she ate the yam because it was one of the few times that Moy has ever put pot to fire.

Friday, October 27

Manman has decided to skip the market tomorrow. Instead we are going to the city to visit my father's sister, Tante Rose.

We have not seen Tante Rose since the summer. Madame Auguste will not have class next week, on All Saints' Day and the Day of the Dead, so we are going to the city. While we are gone, Granmè Melina and Granpè Nozial will look after the fields and the cows for us.

I am glad we are going to see Tante Rose even though I don't especially like the city.

"There is city family and there is country family," Manman often says. "Granmè Melina and Granpè Nozial are your country family. Tante Rose is city family."

Tante Rose comes to visit us in the summer, but never stays for long. She does not like that we have remained in Beau Jour when we could be living in Port-au-Prince.

When Tante Rose was my age, she left the mountains and went to live with a family in the capital. After a few months the family threw her out, so she went to live in an orphanage. The people who ran the orphanage sent her to school. She studied hard and became a nurse.

Papa used to brag a lot about Tante Rose. If anyone asked about Tante Rose — people who still remembered her from when she was a girl — Papa would answer, "My sister is working at the General Hospital in Port-au-Prince, curing the sick."

When the men who used to work with Papa in the fields wanted to tease him, they would say, "Victor, you do not look like you have a sister who is a nurse. You are a peasant. You have big dusty toes. Why would you stay here and live like this when you have a sister in the city?"

People never understand why anyone would choose to stay in the mountains when they could be living in the city.

I can see many advantages myself to living in the mountains as opposed to the city. For one, there are fewer people here. When Manman, Moy, and I go to the capital, I always feel like I am being pushed and shoved by crowds of people. Even when we are in a taxi with Tante Rose, there are always people surrounding the taxi.

"People get lost in the city," Manman says. Not lost in the same way people usually get lost when they are looking for a place they cannot find. People in the city, Manman says, know where they are going, but they still feel lost, as though they are looking for themselves.

No, the mountain does not have an advanced school yet. Moy has to go to Léogâne to attend his tailoring classes. But all in all, like Manman and Papa, I love these mountains, the vetiver and citronella plants along the trails, the rain tapping on the tin roof, even the fog that shifts from place to place in the afternoons.

I love the rainbows during sun showers. I love the shortcuts through the cornfields, the smell of pinewood burning, the golden-brown sap dripping into the fire. I love sleeping on a sisal mat on the clay floor in Granmè Melina and Granpè Nozial's one-room house, and eating in their yard while listening to Granpè Nozial's stories.

We walked down the mountain to Léogâne and found a *tap tap* that was just filling up. There is a hibiscus garden painted on the sides of the *tap tap* and a red flamingo in the middle of the garden. The *tap tap* is a painted camion. They call it a *tap tap* because people tap on the side twice — sometimes more — to signal that they want to get off. Many *tap taps* have names. The one we are in is called Wyclef, and on the front is a phrase in English — "Your love is my love."

I wanted to ask Moy what he thought of the decorations on our *tap tap*, but he seemed far away in his thoughts. He must be thinking about Port-au-Prince and all the things he will do once he gets there.

Moy loves the city. When he is there, he looks at everything as though with new eyes. I am sure he will be more interested in the *tap taps* once we get to Port-au-Prince.

Now and then, Moy's friend Bòs Dezi is hired to paint a *tap tap* in Léogâne. Moy has helped him on some, so it is possible that Moy has painted part of the *tap tap* we are in, or at least one of the others we'll see on our way to Port-au-Prince.

Manman arranged with the driver for three seats. I

chose the window. We were bringing some yams for Tante Rose, which we fit under our seats.

As the *tap tap* became more and more crowded, I looked out of the window, watching all the vendors of colas, peeled sugar cane, fried plantains, fried pork, and sausages. I wanted to have a piece of sugarcane, but I did not dare ask Manman. If I bought the sugarcane, after chewing the juice out, I would have to throw the pulp out of the window sometime during the ride and Manman hated when people did that. It would dirty the road, especially since it was a recently repaved road, and it was thanks to this repaved road that the usual time of the trip to Port-au-Prince would be cut by half. That is, until we reached all the *blokis* within the city limits, in Carrefour. Whenever we go to the capital, the traffic starts piling up in Carrefour, all the way to the bus depot in Port-au-Prince.

Manman was sleeping by the time we reached Carrefour, where everything slowed down, just as I had expected. Moy, on the other hand, was springing to life again, watching everyone and everything.

There were more *tap taps* in Carrefour. Some of them had long phrases written on the sides, words that were designed as beautifully as the pictures.

There were declarations of love — *Sophie, Je t'aime. Marlène, I love you* — and proverbs such as: "The empty sack does not stand," "Sweet syrup draws ants," and "Little yams make a big pile." I liked that last one most of all because I was beginning to feel like Manman, Moy, and me were tiny yams in a very big pile.

Carrefour was full of shops, all with their own beautiful signs: beauty shops, mechanics' shops, schools everywhere, often next to colorful lottery sheds announcing winning lottery numbers. Carrefour was loud, too, with music blasting from some of the stores and a general noise of hundreds of people talking at the same time.

Soon after I got used to all the noise, I fell asleep. The next thing I remember is Manman shaking me to say we had arrived at the bus depot in downtown Port-au-Prince.

Later

Tante Rose was excited to see us, nearly jumping for joy as she embraced each of us.

Tante Rose is not married and she has no children. Two young nurses who work with her at the hospital rent rooms from her. There is a young man who looks after her house when Tante Rose is not at home, as well as a woman who cooks for her and washes her clothes. That woman, Esther, has a daughter, Nadine, who is about my age and who lives in the house, too. Nadine is her mother's shadow and helps her with everything.

Whenever I am in Tante Rose's house, I always think that if Manman moved to the city to work, it would be like that with her and me. She would work in someone's house and I would help her with her work.

Even with the workers and renters, Tante Rose has two rooms left for us. The room I am sharing with Manman has a soft bed. Moy is staying in a smaller room near the living room.

Unlike Papa, Tante Rose is not interested in leaving Haiti. She has her work, which she likes very much, and she enjoys her house, which she had built piece by piece, room by room over many years.

Sunday, October 29

I went up on Tante Rose's roof this morning. From the rooftop, you can see a lot of the capital: the seaport, the presidential palace, the markets downtown, and even the airport.

In the afternoon, Tante Rose took us to Champs de Mars to see a karate movie Moy wanted to see. I liked some of the fights in the movie because they seemed like a dance.

My favorite part of the outing was after the movie when we happened on a concert near the national palace. The music was full of guitars and drums, and there was a line of women dancing on the stage as they sang the choruses.

Tante Rose and Moy danced together in the back of the crowd. Moy likes Tante Rose a lot. When they are together, it is as though they are the same age: Moy acts a lot older than he is and Tante Rose acts a lot younger than she is.

I am beginning to like Port-au-Prince.

Later

We call Papa from Tante Rose's house. After he speaks to Tante Rose, Manman, and Moy, it is my turn.

Papa's voice sounds so warm, like heated milk with cacao when he says, "Celiane."

I say, "How are you, Papa?"

"I am well," he says. "How is school?"

"School is fine," I say.

I was still tongue-tied when I gave the phone back to Manman. I plan for so long about what to say to Papa, but put him on the phone and what comes out, *anyen*, nothing.

Tante Rose, who heard me mention school, says, "Soon you will have to come to school here in the city. That is unless you go to New York first, of course. I want you to know that your papa is not the only one who can help. I have a friend at the consulate who is going to make a special exception for the three of you and get you to New York much faster."

Monday, October 30

I realize now why Manman came to the city. It was only partly to visit with Tante Rose. Last night at supper, she told Tante Rose that she's been feeling more tired than usual, and has been having headaches, and she wants Tante Rose to have a look at her.

"Aline, I am not a doctor," Tante Rose says. "You must see a doctor."

So then and there it was decided. Manman will go to the hospital with Tante Rose this morning and have one of Tante Rose's doctor friends examine her.

Later

I wanted to go to the hospital with Manman, but she said no. As soon as Manman and Tante Rose left for the hospital, Moy went off to buy some paint for Bòs Dezi. To pass the time and to keep myself from worrying too much about Manman, I made the beds, reviewed my lessons, and then went downstairs to help Esther and Nadine prepare the midday meal.

Later

Manman said the doctor told her she had something called *anemi*, or "tired blood." Manman will get better if she eats more green vegetables, like watercress, with lots of liver. The doctor also prescribed tablets for Manman to take every day.

Wednesday, November 1

Moy left for home this morning. He took the paints to Bòs Dezi, who needed them for a sign. Manman wanted us to go back with Moy, but Tante Rose insisted she stay and rest for one more day while Esther and Nadine cooked her some liver and watercress.

It was useless to hope that Manman could rest with Moy gone. She was so worried about him getting into trouble that even though she was lying down, she never slept. At the end of the day, she said she would have gotten more rest if she had gone with Moy, and I agreed.

Today and tomorrow are days when we honor the dead. This morning I saw Tante Rose kneeling before a single lit candle on her dresser.

She was looking up at the candle and speaking to it.

"Manman and Papa," she was saying. "I salute you."

I never knew my father's parents. They both died before I was born. There were no pictures of them, so

I didn't know what they looked like. But when I saw Tante Rose kneeling there, I could almost feel them in the room because I knew she had their faces in her mind as she was talking.

I was watching for a while when Tante Rose turned around and saw me.

"Would you like to say something to them?" she asked.

I went over and kneeled next to her.

"Granmè, Granpè, I wish I had known you," I said.

"You don't know them but they know you," Tante Rose said.

Tante Rose believes the dead are always watching over us and this is her way of honoring her dead parents, just as Granmè Melina cleans her parents' graves every year on the Day of the Dead to honor them.

During All Saints' Day and the Day of the Dead, some people bring flowers and food to the cemeteries where their loved ones are buried. Others go to Mass and pray for their souls. Some musical bands go out in the streets and into the cemeteries. Tante Rose only lights her one candle.

Later

While Manman is in bed, I spend the day listening to the radio. Aside from Christmas songs — radio stations start playing Christmas songs in October — all I hear about is politics. There is going to be a presidential election on November 26th, so whenever you listen to the radio or watch television, all people talk about is politics.

There are seven candidates running for president. The most popular candidate is the former president Jean-Bertrand Aristide. He was president nine years ago, but the Haitian army forced him out through a coup d'état. He spent three years in exile in the United States, then returned in 1994 with help from American forces.

President Aristide stayed in power for one more year and then his time ran out. We had another president for five years, but now President Aristide is a candidate again. His posters are plastered all over Bel-Air. His motto is, *Lapè nan tèt, lapè nan vant,* "Peace in the head, peace in the belly." Everyone is talking about him on the radio, even though he has not been seen in public since early October.

I feel like an outsider to these political discussions

because where I live, people don't talk about politics all that much. Or maybe they do and I am not allowed to go to those places where people gather to do it.

Manman never talks about politics. If someone asks her opinion about an elected official, all she says is, "I don't get involved in politics."

Tante Rose is different. Ask her about the upcoming elections and she says, "If someone is going to do something good for the country, I will get behind that person."

So while Manman lies in bed, I spend my day listening to people discuss politics on the radio. Some people think President Aristide will be reelected and they are glad. Others are still upset about a parliamentary election that took place last May and feel that the results were fixed so President Aristide's party, the Lavalas Family Party, could win. It's so much to think about that while Manman is getting rid of her headache, I am getting one myself.

Thursday, November 2

We are leaving today. Tante Rose took a taxi with us and dropped us off at the bus depot on her way to work.

While we wait for the camion to fill up, vendors come up to the window and Manman buys things from them. So far she has bought a new mesh for our lamp, canned milk, and a straw hat for Granpè Nozial.

Manman never buys anything without bargaining. She and the vendors go back and forth until Manman offers a price the vendor likes. And even when Manman is satisfied with the price, she pretends to be unhappy, as if her hand was forced.

Later

I hope the camion leaves soon. A good number of people are on now. There is a girl my age standing at the window trying to sell chewing gum to Manman. Manman does not want to buy the gum because she says she does not *need* it.

"Buy it for your daughter," the girl says.

Manman sternly replies, "*Non.*"

The girl at the window is insisting. Manman finally buys the gum from her. Manman gives it to me because she does not like gum. I don't like gum, either, but I unwrap the pack and throw each stick into my mouth, one after another, so glad I am that the girl made the sale.

Later

Finally, the camion is leaving.

Nou prale.

NOU PRALE!

We are going.

WE ARE GOING!

Later? Much later?

I am not sure what day it is. The last thing I remember is being on the camion with Manman. In Carrefour. That's right, Carrefour. There was a loud noise. A BANG. Screams. Then everything went black.

Next Day

I am in a hospital, in one long room that smells like alcohol. My head hurts when I try to move it. My wrists ache, too, as I write this. I feel like I am floating, but I surely see that I am in a hospital bed. When I woke up I found you, sweet little book, next to me on the bed.

Later

I sleep a lot. What day is it? WHERE IS MANMAN? I look over at the other beds in the room. There are people of different ages in this room, but only two kids. They are younger than I am, both boys.

If I move my neck too fast, it hurts. I have no bandages, just a bump the size of a baby's fist on the back of my head and a few cuts and bruises along my arms and legs. It does not feel like I have any broken bones (though I have never broken any bones before). I feel like I have been thrown about and have had my arms and legs stretched too far, like an old rag doll. I want to know what happened to Manman. I see a nurse at the other end of the room. I scream, "Manman! Manman!"

The nurse walks over to me. She looks at a paper in her hand and says, "Just rest."

I remember Tante Rose wanting Manman to rest. Then I ask again, "Where is my Manman?"

"I see you found your book," she says, "It was inside your blouse when you came here. You were holding on to it so tightly."

"Is my Manman well?" I ask.

"I don't know," she says.

Sunday, November 5

I asked the nurse what day it was and she told me. I hear church bells in the distance. Some of the patients who are able to get up walk back and forth through the louvered doors where the sun is coming in. Even though I feel as though I can walk fine, I have no desire to see outside. I just want to see Manman.

Later

Another nurse spoke to me this afternoon. She asked me my name and where I live. I told her about Tante Rose and where she works.

"So your head is fine," she said. "You know who you are. We were afraid you wouldn't. Your family is probably looking for you. People who survived that explosion were lucky."

"An explosion?" Even though I had heard that bang, I thought it was a collision, that a bigger camion had hit ours from behind.

"It was a pipe bomb," the nurse said, "something to do with the elections."

She said there was a shooting in the capital at the same time, also related to the elections. Gunmen wounded five people at a bus depot.

"You are safe here," she said. "There will be no explosions and no shootings here."

Even as she was saying this, she didn't look or sound very certain.

Monday, November 6

I can sit up in bed now if I try. I ask the nurse about Manman every time she brings me food. She simply tells me to rest. I do not remember Tante Rose's telephone number. I don't think I ever knew it. Manman and Moy always made all the calls to her house from the Teleco in Léogâne.

Tuesday, November 7

Why haven't Tante Rose and Manman and Moy found me yet? Have the nurses let Tante Rose know I am here?

Wednesday, November 8

I will not let myself think the worst about Manman. Dear, sweet little book, if I could hold on to you so tightly that you are now here with me, why couldn't I have done the same for Manman?

Thursday, November 9

Tante Rose and Moy look like visions when they arrive, like the animal forms that clouds sometimes take in the sky. I never realized that happiness could make people appear so airy and light. Tante Rose and Moy seemed to be floating, like sheets in the breeze. Was I dreaming them again? If so, why weren't Manman and Papa standing there with them the way they were in all my dreams?

Tante Rose held my hand and cried.

"I should have let you and Aline leave with Moy like you planned," she said.

Moy was standing a few steps away, fighting back his tears.

"Is Manman alive?" I asked Tante Rose.

"We are going to take you to see her," Tante Rose said.

Later

Manman cried, too, when she saw me, except she cried much longer than Tante Rose did. As soon as Moy carried me into the house and put me down on the bed, Manman lay down next to me and just cried and cried and cried. At times she sobbed loudly. Other times she just moaned and said, "I don't know what I would have done . . . I don't know what I would have done . . ."

I was so happy to see Manman that I wanted to reach up and kiss her, but she wouldn't let me move. She wouldn't even let me speak.

Friday, November 10

Manman seems all right except she walks with a limp. Tante Rose took both our temperatures before she left for work this morning.

My body is aching less now after a full day of everyone looking after me, Nadine and Esther making me soup and tea, Manman rubbing my arms and legs with castor oil, and Moy peeking into the room now and then to check on me.

Saturday, November 11

Manman has finally allowed me to leave the room, but Moy follows me everywhere with a worried look on his face. This is all new to Moy, the frightening part of the city.

The bump on the back of my head has shrunk some. Even though I am not trying to listen, I over-hear Manman and Tante Rose discussing whether they should call Papa and tell him what happened.

Manman thinks it's best that Papa does not know what happened as he would worry.

"Victor will be mad when he hears that we kept this from him," Tante Rose says.

"We are alive," Manman says. "That's all he needs to know."

Sunday, November 12

I went up on Tante Rose's roof when no one was looking. I wanted to be outside, to look up at the sky, and see the mountains in the distance. Despite the shootings and the pipe bombs, people are still going about their lives, walking to and from church, visiting with friends and family.

Monday, November 13

This afternoon while Manman and Tante Rose were in another part of the house, Moy came into the bedroom to see how I was doing. I took the opportunity to ask him some questions, to help me fill in the void between the time of the explosion and the time I woke up in the hospital.

Moy was in Léogâne, in class, when the explosion happened. After his class someone told him that a bomb had hit a camion in Carrefour. He knew we were coming back that same day and, even if we were not in the camion that had been hit, we would be stuck in Carrefour anyway, so he went there immediately to see if he could find us.

By the time he reached Carrefour, all the accident victims had been taken away. Moy thought that we had gotten through earlier and had gone home, so he headed to Beau Jour. When he got to Beau Jour late into the night, he saw that we were not there, so he went back to Léogâne the next morning and called Tante Rose on the telephone to see if we had stayed with her.

Tante Rose and Moy went to all the hospitals in Port-au-Prince, Carrefour, and Léogâne. They found Manman at a hospital in Carrefour, but they couldn't find me. They looked for me every day. They even had an announcement made on the radio. Manman was beside herself, crying day and night. They never thought I would be taken to a small private clinic as far south as Carrefour Dufort. Then one of the nurses from the clinic called Tante Rose at work to tell her where I was. A driver in a private car had picked up the two boys and me and had taken us there.

"Manman's leg seems hurt," I said.

"She has a cut on her calf," Moy said. "Glass from the explosion. She doesn't want you to know about it. She doesn't want you to worry."

"I want to go back to Beau Jour," I said. "When are we going back?"

"I don't know," Moy said. "Tante Rose wants Manman's cut to heal before she leaves. Tante Rose says that losing blood from the cut will make Manman's *anemi* worse, so she has to stay here and take her tablets while building up her strength. Otherwise she might get light-headed on the trip up the mountain. Besides, Manman is afraid to travel through Carrefour again."

Tuesday, November 14

We all gather at night to watch the television news broadcasts. Some of the presidential candidates are asking for the November 26th election to be postponed after protesters tried to burn down four electoral offices.

Wednesday, November 15

I saw the bandage on Manman's leg as she was getting dressed this morning. It runs from the back of her knee down to her lower calf. I know her wound hasn't healed yet because she grimaces sometimes while walking.

Later

Moy went to the bus depot to find someone to send word to Granmè Melina and Granpè Nozial that we were staying in the city longer. Moy says that the word will be passed on through at least four people before it reaches Granmè Melina and Granpè Nozial, but it will get to them.

Thursday, November 16

Another shooting. Gunmen in a pickup truck fired at people at a bus depot last night. No one was hurt, miraculously. Another miracle: it was not the same bus depot that Moy had gone to.

Some men in the neighborhood are setting up

roadblocks to keep cars away so these same kinds of shootings don't happen on our streets.

Moy went out to help. Manman did not want him to go, but Moy went anyway. I am proud of Moy for trying to protect us.

Later

We wait for Moy to return. When he does, he smells of gasoline, tar, smoke, and sweat. At nineteen, Moy is already a man. His gaze is becoming more resolved, more determined, all the time. He is looking more and more like Papa.

Friday, November 17

Tante Rose still goes to work every day. We worry about her while she is gone. Moy spends his days sketching and Manman spends most of hers next to me in the bed that Tante Rose insists we both remain in.

I almost know my history book by heart now. Sometimes I recite my lessons to Manman and she likes that. What she likes most are those lessons about the battle of independence when Haitians came together to fight French colonists and form our nation. "Where are these kinds of people now?" Manman said at the end of one of those lessons. "Now all we do is fight each other over elections, put bombs in cars to blow up women and children."

Manman got so upset that tears streamed down her face.

I wish the people who throw the bombs at the buses could see that not only do they hurt the bodies of people like Manman and me, they wound our souls, too.

Later

Tonight while watching the television news broadcast, we heard gunfire in the distance. What kind of bad news will the morning bring?

Saturday, November 18

There was no electricity today, so we listened to Christmas songs on Tante Rose's battery-powered radio. We avoided the political programs altogether.

This is the time of the month that Papa sends us a cassette. I miss sitting in the front room with Manman and Moy listening to Papa's voice.

Sunday, November 19

Every couple of days, Tante Rose changes the dressing on Manman's wound. Manman is taking her tablets daily and seems to only eat watercress and liver. She must really want to get better quickly so we can go home.

Monday, November 20

Moy made a drawing of Manman and me lying in bed together. I am reading to Manman from my history book. It must have been a war-free passage because in the drawing, Manman is listening calmly with her eyes closed.

Moy's drawing is so beautiful and so real that as I look at it I feel as though I am in the moment again, lying there with Manman and reading to her. I realize now what is magical about what Moy does. His pictures give you a chance to relive something, as though you had stepped out of your own skin for a while.

Moy and Manman are no longer speaking to one another in strained voices. Even when Manman scolds Moy about going to play dominoes with the boys across the street, it sounds more like she is making a suggestion than giving him orders. Moy tells Manman he needs to pass the time somehow, making it sound as though he would like to obey Manman, but has no choice but to go out and play with the neighborhood boys. Even though I am not trying to listen, I hear Manman complain to Tante Rose that Moy is getting to know too many of the boys in the neighborhood.

"Moy has always been good at making friends quickly," Tante Rose says. "That's one of his charms."

Tuesday, November 21

The National Police arrested thirteen people who were involved in plotting and carrying out the shootings and bombings. They promised that there would be more arrests.

Among the people who were interviewed on the

television news broadcast tonight, some thought President Aristide's party was responsible for the violence. Others thought the opposition was to blame.

Wednesday, November 22

A teenage boy was killed, another bomb victim. All in all, seven pipe bombs exploded in the city today.

Thursday, November 23

A seven-year-old girl was killed. She was on a bus, on her way to school. A bomb was thrown at her bus. The girl was killed in Carrefour, where our camion was hit.

This really makes me angry. Why must children be killed? They are not involved in politics.

Friday, November 24

Tante Rose was so sad when she came home. Both she and the other nurses looked very tired.

"We had a hard day," Tante Rose said, "but not as hard as the people we treated."

She did not want to watch the evening news broadcast.

"I have already seen more than I can bear," she said.

Saturday, November 25

President Aristide visited the spot where the boy was killed by a bomb. Manman leaned closer to the television screen to get a better look at President Aristide as he knelt down and kissed the ground.

Later

Papa called. He had been hearing about the bombings all the way in New York and wanted to tell Tante Rose to be careful. He was surprised to find out that we were at her house.

When Manman got on the phone, she told him everything.

I could tell by the way Manman was talking that it took a lot of reassuring words to calm Papa down. His face was probably changing, the way it did when he watched the stars fall out of the sky.

After he and Manman had spoken for a while, he asked to talk to Moy, who assured him again that we were okay.

When my turn came, I couldn't hold back.

"I am afraid, Papa," I said. "I want to go to Beau Jour, but we cannot because there are bombs on the road and Manman's leg is hurt."

"Don't be afraid, Cécé," Papa said. "I am working very hard so you and Moy and Manman can come to New York and we can spend Christmas together. My friend Franck is a rich man here. He is doing a lot to help us."

And just like that, I was less afraid. Papa's voice could always calm my fears. Even when I was little and would wake up screaming in the middle of the night thinking I had heard Galipòt galloping up to our front door, Papa would whisper in the dark, "Cécé, many things like Galipòt exist in the streams of our dreams, but they cannot hurt us."

That's when I knew that nothing that was happening now could hurt us. Neither the elections, nor the shootings, nor the bombings.

Sunday, November 26
Election Day. 8:00 A.M.

It's quiet this morning. No sounds of gunfire or loud voices on the street discussing the bombings and shootings, who is responsible for them, and how to stop them.

Everyone in the house is dressed and walking about, but no one is going out.

I walked into the living room and found Tante Rose sitting alone between the television and the radio, both turned off, because of another power outage and worn-out radio batteries.

"Are you feeling well, Tante Rose?" I asked her.

"I am trying to decide if I should vote," she said.

"Will you vote?" I asked.

"I am deciding," she said. "You see, Cécé, the year you were born, in 1987, there was another election. You were born in January and the election was in November 1987. It was the country's first election in thirty years. Everyone was so excited to go out to vote, but when the polling stations opened, the military shot and killed thirty-four people. They threw grenades into the streets, destroyed radio stations. It was a very bad time. When the killings happened, I told myself that whenever I could I would vote for the people who had died at those polling stations that day. I have not missed a vote yet."

12:00 P.M.

The power is still out, but Raymond, the young man who looks after the house when Tante Rose is away, found some fresh batteries for Tante Rose's radio. We are all gathered around the radio, even the two nurses, along with Nadine and Esther.

Raymond keeps switching back and forth between radio stations. As soon as a report is done on one station, he immediately moves on to another.

There are many reporters doing broadcasts directly from the polling stations, interviewing people as they come in to vote. It doesn't seem as though a lot of people are voting. The radio reporters said that the lines were very short.

This morning before a polling station opened in Carrefour, a bomb exploded there, injuring one man. Aside from that there have been no other acts of violence.

"This is not the same kind of election we had in 1990," Tante Rose said.

President Aristide had been elected for the first time in 1990. During that election, the lines were very long, stretching back further than the eye could see. People waited for hours to vote, some arriving at the polling stations before dawn and leaving late into the night. Once they had voted, they went into the streets to dance and show off the purple ink their fingers had been dipped in to keep them from voting again. They tore off tree branches and waved them in the air while singing carnival hymns. Voters flooded the capital from all the provinces. Some Haitians came back from France, Canada, and the United States to cast ballots.

To hear Tante Rose tell it, it was a beautiful day.

"Did you vote then, Tante Rose?" Moy asked.

"Of course I did," Tante Rose said. "I am also going to vote today."

So she had made up her mind.

"Don't waste your time, Rose," Manman said. "None of those politicians are going to do anything for the country."

"Aline, you think you live in a different country

where you are up in the mountains?" Tante Rose said. "It's the same country. We all live in the same country."

"Then why don't you tell that to your politicians when you go out and vote for them," Manman said. "They never think about the people in the mountains. Victor had to leave so we would not eat dust up there. I vote for Victor, my husband. He is my president."

Manman got up and limped away, grimacing in pain as she went. I started to follow her, but she waved her hand, signaling for me to stay back.

2:00 P.M.

Complete silence among us now as we listen to radio reports from the polling stations. Manman still has not come out of the room. Tante Rose and one of the nurses are about to go out and vote.

"I want to go, too," Moy whispers so Manman won't hear.

"Are you registered, Moy?" Tante Rose asks.

"In Léogâne," he says. "Manman doesn't know."

"You must vote in Léogâne then," Tante Rose says.

"I just want to go with you," Moy says.

"All right then," Tante Rose says. "Let's go quickly. It's not far away."

I can't believe Tante Rose is encouraging Moy to defy Manman. She must know that this is going to cause problems with Manman. As she is tiptoeing out of the house with Moy and the nurse, Tante Rose puts a finger over her mouth, signaling for me to be quiet.

3:00 P.M.

As soon as Moy and Tante Rose left, I went up to the roof to have a look at the street. There were not as many people walking around as usual, except a few who were heading home from church or coming back from voting, or both.

All of a sudden, a shriek from downstairs. I rush down there. It's Manman.

"Where is Moy?" she asks.

"Out with Tante Rose," I say.

"Voting?" Manman holds her head with both hands as if to keep it from exploding.

"That woman!" shouts Manman. "We must leave this house. We cannot stay here anymore."

Manman limps back to the room and drops herself on the bed.

"We have to stay for your leg," I remind her.

"I know," Manman says. "That woman and this leg are holding me prisoner here. We should have never come. Look what it has brought us."

She raises her skirt to show me the bandage and then pulls back the bandage slowly to show the cut. It was larger and deeper than I had feared. It still must hurt a lot because Manman moans in pain at night and grimaces when she walks.

In spite of the way the wound looks and how much it frightens me, I say, "It could have been worse, Manman. We both could have died, like those children."

"I know," Manman says, resigning herself to having to stay in Tante Rose's house a while longer.

Today more than most days, I wish Papa were here to console Manman, to reassure her more than I ever could.

5:00 P.M.

Manman and I are waiting in the living room when Tante Rose and Moy and the other nurse return.

Manman's face relaxes a little bit when she sees that they are all right.

"Sister," Tante Rose says, walking toward Manman, "the streets are empty. It was safe."

"Sister," Manman says, "since you call me sister. Just because I am in your house and you are looking after me does not make my children your own."

8:30 P.M.

The evening news reports say that fewer people came out to vote than were expected. Perhaps it was because, like Manman, they worried about possible violence and were afraid.

Monday, November 27

The city is back to normal. I could make it all out from Tante Rose's roof: the reopened shops, the street vendors, cars lined up behind one another in traffic jams, horns blowing from every direction.

Manman and Tante Rose are friendly again. They exchanged a few jokes while Tante Rose looked over Manman's leg this morning.

Papa called while I was still asleep to check on us. Manman said he sounded calmer, less worried.

Tuesday, November 28

Moy decided to go back to Beau Jour. Manman tried to convince him to stay, but he said he needed to see about the cornfields and the cows, which Granpè Nozial and Granmè Melina have been looking after since we left.

I know the camion trip back will be very difficult for Manman and I want to be with her when she decides to make it.

Manman resigned herself to the fact that Moy would go without us, so she told Moy to pick up Papa's cassette and the money at the transfer place. She said nothing about when she thought she would be able to go home.

I realize now just how afraid Manman is of traveling through Carrefour. This is probably why she is leaving with Moy in spite of her leg. I, too, am afraid of being in another camion and having the same thing happen.

Some nights I dream that after the bombing I am

lost and never found again, that I forget my name, and am unable to tell anyone who I am. Other nights I dream that it is Manman who is lost and who forgets her name and is never found.

I had these same types of dreams after Papa left, that he would get to New York and find a new son and daughter and a new wife and forget about us.

Wednesday, November 29

President Aristide is officially declared the winner of the election. On the television news broadcast, they said he received two million votes.

Thursday, November 30

I am feeling much better now. The bump on my head is no more and my bruises have faded into little scars that hardly show. I am saying prayers every day that soon Manman can say the same.

Friday, December 1

It's already been a month since we've been here. If we're here any longer, we might as well stay for Christmas.

This morning, I saw Manman walking back and forth across the room, as if trying to will her leg to do exactly what she wants it to do.

I think the leg is getting better. She moans less at night and grimaces less often when she walks.

Saturday, December 2

We are home! I am writing by the light of our kerosene lamp. Everyone is asleep. The cooking rocks are still warm from the fire and I could spend all night staring at the cinders in the ashes when I am not looking up at the stars.

When we woke up this morning, Manman said, "We are leaving today. I am tired of Rose's house. I want to go back to my own house."

She announced this to Tante Rose as soon as Tante Rose woke up.

"I feel bad that I made you stay longer the last time," Tante Rose said. "I am not going to tell you to stay this time, even though I think you should wait for your leg to heal completely, but if you must go, let me take you."

Tante Rose told Raymond to find her a car. An hour later, Raymond came back with a borrowed car and we were off.

Manman and I sat together in the back. Tante Rose sat up front while Raymond drove.

As we neared Carrefour, Tante Rose asked Raymond to use a shortcut off the main road to spare Manman from having to see the bombing site again. Raymond did this and in no time we were in Léogâne.

Once we got there, Tante Rose rented two mules. Manman rode one with her hurt leg stretched out in front of her, just as Tante Rose recommended. Tante Rose and I rode the other mule. By late afternoon, we were finally home.

Sunday, December 3

I thought Tante Rose would rush back to the city early in the morning, but she did not. She went with Moy to see the fields and Papa's cows, then stayed for the midday meal Granmè Melina cooked for us.

Granmè Melina and Granpè Nozial were thrilled to see us. I couldn't stop staring at them, I was so happy. As usual, Granmè Melina smelled like coffee. I didn't realize how much I missed that smell and how much I missed her.

As we ate, Grandpè Nozial told us a story about a man who left the mountain to go to the city and in the city discovered ice. The man liked ice so much he wanted to bring some back up the mountain, but by the time he got up the mountain with the ice, the ice had melted. The man came back to the village several times and tried to find a way to define ice to his friends, who had never seen it, but all he had to show for his encounter with the ice was a wet shirt. "So ice is a wet shirt," his friends told the man to keep him from feeling too bad.

I think the lesson of the story is that even though Granpè Nozial hadn't been to the city with us to see for himself what we had been through, he could understand it because he could see the result in Manman's leg.

Granpè Nozial can always think of a story to make you feel better, no matter how strange the story.

After the meal, Tante Rose showed Moy and me

how to change the dressing on Manman's leg, and she made us promise that we would remind Manman to take her tablets and eat plenty of green vegetables and liver when she could find it. Tante Rose also ordered us not to let Manman go down to the market until her leg was completely healed.

Tante Rose said she would have a surprise for us when she saw us again at Christmas. I asked her what it was, but she refused to tell me. She can be quite a torturer, that Tante Rose, saying something like that just as Moy starts walking her down the mountain.

Monday, December 4

It feels wonderful to be back in school. Madame Auguste made me stand as she made a welcoming speech in my honor.

"We're happy Celiane is with us again," she said. "We missed her. Did we not miss her, class?"

There were some whispers, but I think almost everyone missed me except Pouchon, who's been in first place since I have been gone.

During recess, Thérèse prodded me for details

about my adventures in the city. At times during my telling, Thérèse was frightened and outraged. At other times she was plain jealous that I got to spend all that time in the city, no matter how dangerous it was.

She wanted to know how Moy had handled himself. I told her he did well. We couldn't have gotten along without him, I said. This seemed to increase her esteem for Moy and I think for me, too.

Tuesday, December 5

Madame Auguste had a special lesson about Christophe Colomb, the Italian explorer who came to our island on this day in 1492 from Spain.

Before Colomb arrived, there were Arawak Indians living here and plenty of gold mines. Colomb and his men made the Arawaks work the gold mines and exposed them to diseases from Europe, to which the Arawaks had no resistance.

Soon, all the Arawaks died.

After Colomb and his men left, the French came and imported slaves from Africa. Most Haitians, Madame Auguste says, are the descendants of those slaves.

Wednesday, December 6

Manman has visitors all the time, friends who come by to see how she is doing. They bring food and all kinds of teas and home remedies for her.

Tonight after the last person left, we listened to the cassette that Papa sent us while we were in the city. He said that his friend Franck had written another letter and had made some calls to the consulate in Haiti to ask if we could be allowed to come to New York sooner.

Monday, December 11

I have been spending so much time catching up with my studies I haven't been able to write. Manman is doing much better. She has been walking with much less difficulty. All the country medicine mixed in with Tante Rose's city medicine must be helping.

Wednesday, December 13

Christmas is quickly approaching. My classmates will be performing a Nativity play on Christmas Eve. I am not going to be in the play because they began rehearsals while I was gone. Thérèse will be Mary and Pouchon will play Joseph.

To make me feel included, Thérèse keeps asking my opinions on everything, how she should say her lines, how she should wear her hair, etc. . . .

Thérèse has sewn a rag doll to stand in as the baby Jesus. Some men from our village will build the manger and the star. The other pupils will play the innkeepers, shepherds, angels, and the three wise men.

I cannot wait for Christmas Eve. Manman will make her delicious coconut drink, *kremas*, along with codfish fritters. Granpè Nozial and Granmè Melina will come over and will stay up all night talking, while Granpè Nozial throws rock salt into the cooking fire to set off sparks. Moy will finally finish his *fanal*, a cardboard lantern built in the shape of a *tap tap*, which he will hang in front of the house.

If there is a bright moon, some of the boys from the surrounding villages might come to our yard to show off their own *fanals*. As they leave to go down the mountain to another house, carrying *fanals* of various shapes and sizes, they will look like a giant necklace of fireflies.

Manman says the *fanals* help Tonton Nwèl, Father

Christmas, find the houses where there are children. But if the children are bad, the light also brings the old man with the whip, Papa Fwèt. Unlike Father Christmas, who leaves presents under children's pillows, Papa Fwèt cracks his whip loudly and frightens them into being good next year.

Friday, December 15

Who should come to see us but Tante Rose? She says we are going to have a Christmas miracle. She has been talking to her contact at the American consulate. We have to go there Monday and if all goes well, we should be able to join Papa in New York by Christmas.

"I told my contact about you and Celiane almost being killed by that bomb," Tante Rose said. "I showed her the clinic and hospital papers. I begged and begged. Victor's friend Franck wrote another letter, too, and made some phone calls, and it seems the three of you have a good chance of being approved."

I didn't know what to think. Seeing Papa at Christmas? It does not seem possible.

Saturday, December 16

There is so much to do in so little time. The biggest decision: What to do with the house? Granmè Melina and Granpè Nozial are going to look after it and Papa's corn and cows until Manman and Papa can decide what to do with everything. (Manman and Papa together again. What an idea!)

Moy has already picked out what he will be bringing with him to New York. He made a pile in a corner of the front room, his clothes and the notebooks with his sketches in them.

Later

I went to Thérèse's house and asked her mother if Thérèse could spend the afternoon with us. This gives us some time to say good-bye. It will also give Thérèse time to be around Moy, which I know she will like.

I suddenly have a secret wish that Moy will come back to marry Thérèse, so Thérèse will be my sister-in-law. I know it is a silly dream, but it will make it easier for me to part with Thérèse, who before you, sweet little book, I told all my secrets to. But the way

I am feeling now, I cannot even tell Thérèse about it.

There is a part of me that does not want to leave, that is afraid to leave. It is the same part of me that's worried Papa will be a stranger to me when I see him again, that in another country, my family — I mean my whole family, which includes Granmè Melina and Granpè Nozial and Tante Rose, too — will grow much further apart rather than closer together.

I could not tell any of this to Thérèse. If I told her, she would think me ungrateful, even crazy. No one, not even Thérèse, would understand my hesitation. I don't completely understand it myself.

On the way back from Thérèse's house, she and I promised to write to one another. Thérèse's mother will pick up the letters when she goes to Léogâne. Thérèse will keep me up to date on everything that happens here and I will write her of all the new things that happen to me in New York.

We crossed pinkies, swearing we will never forget each other.

Later

Thérèse went back to her house. We will say our final good-bye tomorrow, since we'll have to pass her house on the way down to Léogâne.

Later

The stars are out in large numbers tonight. While Manman and Moy continue packing their things, with help from Granmè Melina and Granpè Nozial, Tante Rose and I sit out in the yard for a while looking up at the stars.

Tante Rose is staring so hard she hardly blinks. Perhaps she is remembering what it was like to look up at this same sky when she was a girl. If I ever come back here as a woman, maybe I will look at the sky in the same way.

Sunday, December 17

We all got up with the first rooster's crow. I never heard the roosters so loudly before. Perhaps it is because I was not sleeping deeply anyway.

Manman's leg seems healed now. Or maybe she

has so many other things to think about that she is not concerned about her leg, but she is walking just like she did before the explosion.

As we packed our things on Granpè Nozial's mule, he told us his ice story again. This time the lesson seemed to be that he was happy enough that we were going to a place he hadn't seen and we need not worry that he would be jealous.

On the way down the mountain, we passed Thérèse's house. I said good-bye to her, renewing our vows to remain friends forever. I held her so tight and for so long that everyone left me behind.

I had to run to catch up. As I ran toward my family, I felt like I was being disloyal to Thérèse, like I was deserting her. I didn't look back because I did not want to cry even more than I already did.

When I caught up with Moy, he pulled a handkerchief from his pocket and gave it to me to wipe my face.

"You'll see her again," he said. "We'll come back to visit her."

I didn't believe Moy. If this were true, then why had Papa never come back to visit us?

I had asked Manman that question once. The answer was that until a few weeks ago, Papa still hadn't been "legal" in America, and if he had come to see us, he would not have been allowed to go back.

Was America a prison that once you entered you were never allowed to leave? Would we be "legal" when we got there?

As we walked the rest of the way down the mountain, (Manman rode the mule so as not to strain her leg) I kept thinking of returning to Beau Jour one day to visit with Granmè Melina, Granpè Nozial, Thérèse, and Madame Auguste, or just to look at the stars the way Tante Rose did last night. This made me feel a little better.

Later

Raymond was waiting for us with the borrowed car after the river crossing in Léogâne. We said good-bye to Granpè Nozial and Granmè Melina before climbing into the car. They did not sniffle or cry. They just told us they would see us soon.

I think this is the proper way of saying good-bye, telling someone you will see her soon. This takes a lot of sadness out of it.

Granpè Nozial and Granmè Melina watched us take our seats in the car and then started back across the river and up the mountain.

Monday, December 18

At the consulate, we were interviewed by a lady with amber eyes and hair like cornhusks. She asked Manman for our documents and examined them and then examined the ones she had in her own dossier.

After reading all the papers, she asked Manman a few questions, like when she and Papa were married and who was there, on what dates Moy and I were born. She then asked who our sponsor was in New York. Tante Rose spoke up and said that Papa's friend Franck, who owned several restaurants in New York, had written many letters and made several phone calls on our behalf.

"All seems to be in order," the lady says. "The only thing is . . ." She looks up at us, then searches the documents for our names. When she finds it, she says, "I need for you, Madame Aline, and for Celiane to have another medical examination."

It was just a precaution, she explained. Since we

had both been hurt in that bombing in Carrefour, she had to make sure we were not going to the United States for medical care we could not afford, for which the city of New York would have to pay.

The woman handed Manman a piece of paper with some doctors' names. As soon as she received the results of our examinations, she said, if all was fine, she would approve our visas and we could travel immediately, if that's what we wanted to do.

After we left her office, we took a taxi to the office of the same doctor who had examined all three of us the year before. Even though he had a long line of patients waiting, Tante Rose used her charms, and the fact that they know some of the same people at the General Hospital, to get him to examine us. He then gave Tante Rose a paper saying we were okay.

Tuesday, December 19

WE ARE APPROVED!

This time, after leaving the consulate, we went directly to the airport to buy our airplane tickets.

We are leaving in two days.

Manman had to borrow money from Tante Rose

for the tickets. They cost a lot more than Manman had because we were leaving so soon.

Wednesday, December 20

This morning, I was sitting in the living room when Tante Rose walked over and put a hand on my shoulder.

"Celiane Espérance," she says in a serious voice, "do you know why I am doing all this, spending every *gourde* I have to see that you and Moy and Aline get to be with Victor? For months and months, I begged my contact at the consulate. Do you know why?"

"Because you are our family," I say.

"That," she says, "and because even when things were very hard for my brother, he never asked me for anything before. This is the first time he's asked me to do something for him. And you know what he asked? To do everything so you and he and Moy and Aline can be together this Christmas."

"Thank you, Tante Rose," I say.

"You don't have to thank me," she says. "I felt so bad that you and Aline were in that camion when the bomb hit it. I want to do this for you."

Thursday, December 21

Raymond drove us to the airport. Everything is happening so fast, I don't know what to think anymore.

I am trying to feel the way I know everyone would want me to feel. Maybe I am lucky. Maybe I am the luckiest girl in Haiti. After five years of separation, I am finally going to see my father.

Still, I can't shake the old fears and new ones, too: What if the plane falls out of the sky? What if we never make it to New York? What if we hate New York? What if we all hate each other when we get to New York?

I have told myself that once I see Papa, I will know in one instant if everything will be all right. If my stomach feels settled when I see him and my fears vanish at the first sight of him, then I will know that everything will be fine.

Later

It seems like the biggest part of traveling is waiting in line. The line to check our bags was very long. It took us two hours to reach the counter where we were assigned our seats. And then it was time to say good-bye to Tante Rose.

As with Granmè Melina and Granpè Nozial, this was a short good-bye.

"Give Victor a kiss for me," Tante Rose said. Then she vanished into the crowd.

I can't help but wonder if I will ever see Tante Rose again.

Later

I am writing this on the airplane. Manman seems uneasy. She has been trembling ever since she got on. Moy is looking out the window. To keep my mind off everything but the present, I have decided to make a list of the things I would have missed had I never been on an airplane.

1. I would have missed the rise — going up, up, up from the ground and floating up in the air, as though inside a bird.
2. I would have missed seeing the clouds in the sky so close.

3. I would have missed watching the plane glide down from the sky and then watching a city appear below, a city filled with ice crystals and light.

New York, U.S.A.

Thursday, December 21
11:30 P.M.

I must write this before I sleep because I never want to forget it as long as I live, our first moment with Papa. It worked. The pact I made with myself worked. As soon as I saw Papa I knew that everything would be all right, that things would fall in place, that we would be okay.

We heard him before we saw him, a deep voice calling our names. We looked around everywhere trying to find him; then all of a sudden he was right there, a few feet away. He hadn't changed much except for some gray hairs and a beard he hadn't had before.

I rushed to him and grabbed him, almost coming up to his chest, which was a little strange since the last time I saw him, I was only as tall as his belly. I couldn't believe he was close enough for me to smell the scent of fresh soap on him, to touch him, to hold him, to see his smile.

When Manman embraced him, she ended up embracing us both. Squeezed between the two of them, I could hear her sobbing.

I removed myself from between them to give Moy a chance to say hello. Moy and Papa shook hands over Manman's shoulder.

Manman had that look in her eyes, too, the look she has only when Papa is around. Her eyes were shining, as though there were little bits of stars in them. It was as if every sad moment she had lived through these past five years, every second that she'd spent missing Papa, had been erased from her memory. She was so happy that even if I still had some doubts, her smile, the tears of joy flowing out of her eyes, would have taken them away.

A man came forward. It was Papa's friend Franck. Manman greeted Franck and thanked him for everything he's done for us.

"Welcome to the Tenth Department," Franck said. (Haiti is made up of nine geographical regions or "departments," and those living abroad, in the Diaspora, are considered part of a tenth one.)

We went outside, where Papa loaded our things into Franck's jeep. It was cold, cold like I have never felt before. There was snow on the ground and more was falling, like mountain rain with rice grain–sized hail, except the snow was falling much more slowly. The wind was blowing it around us and the snow was floating aimlessly, thousands and thousands of tiny clouds, which when the light hit them looked as though they had been dipped in liquid crystal.

I thought of Granpè Nozial's ice story. Granpè Nozial would have loved to see the snow, to watch bits of ice falling out of the sky.

I held out my hands to catch a few snow shavings, but they melted as soon as they touched my palm. Shivering, Manman and Moy rushed into the car, but I stood there watching the soft ice turn to water blots on my fingertips.

Papa reached over and took my hand.

"I was so excited I forgot the coats," he said as he helped me into the backseat where Moy and Manman were huddled together to keep warm.

As we drove out of the airport, Papa reached back and took Manman's hand. The snow kept falling, swirling around the streetlamps and car lights.

There were blinking lights strung over the trees on the roads and highways, houses gleaming with

Christmas wreaths on the front doors, candles and Christmas trees in the windows, life-size Nativity scenes on front lawns, and blown-up Father Christmases riding carriages on rooftops.

"You are wet," Manman said to me.

By now the airport snow had penetrated my clothes. I could even feel the tingle of cold water sliding down my back.

"Cécé, are you cold?" Papa asked.

"Yes, I am," I said, my teeth chattering, "but I am fine."

And I was. Papa was alive to me again. I could feel, hear, touch him. He did not have another family. We were still his only family. Judging from the big smile on in his face, he loved us just as much as he did before, if not even more.

Moy seemed happy, too, looking out of the window, taking in everything. I could finally understand what Tante Rose meant when she said the word "miracle." Our reunion felt even more wondrous than a miracle, a dream too large for even Franck's giant jeep to contain.

Friday, December 22

We slept until noon, then ventured out to see the street. The snow had stopped falling, but there was still a lot of it on the ground.

The street was quiet, the red-bricked row houses lined up like snowcapped soldiers standing at full attention. The snow now seemed to muffle things, even people, who as they walked past us would keep their heads low, close to their chests, their entire bodies covered in layers of thick material, their faces wrapped with scarves, which, even if they were looking at us, would barely allow us to see their eyes.

It suddenly occurred to me that we looked like those people. Papa had gotten us sweaters, knit caps, scarves, coats, and rubber boots that made squishing noises each time we took a step.

Out in the cold, I understood why the people walking past us didn't raise their heads, for each time I raised mine, my nose ran, my eyes watered, and my face twitched as though a million ice needles were being hammered into my skin. Each time I took a step, I kept slipping on ice patches, nearly falling down. Even though the sun was shining, it did nothing to warm me. Instead it seemed allied with the chill, transforming itself into something I never knew existed, a cold sun.

Needless to say, we were only outside for a few minutes. Manman couldn't bear much more than that and pleaded with Papa to take us back inside.

Papa said we would soon get used to the cold, just as he has. But I don't think I will ever get used to this cold that seeps into your body, all the way to your bones.

Later

We live in a two-bedroom apartment on the ground floor of one of the row houses owned by Franck. Manman and Papa have the larger bedroom and I have a smaller one next to theirs. Poor Moy is sleeping in the front room again.

We are waiting for a larger apartment upstairs which will become available at the end of February. Then Moy will finally have his own room.

After our brief trip outside, we spent the afternoon cooking and talking. Papa wanted to hear about everything that's happened in Beau Jour since he's been gone. He had so many questions that even before we finished answering one question, he already had another. It seemed like he asked about everyone and everything he's ever known.

Moy appeared to enjoy answering the questions the most because he was finally getting to speak to Papa, face-to-face, man to man. I feel as though I can see inside Moy's head. There must be something in him that feels complete now, just like something in me feels whole, like a piece of me that's been missing for five years has finally been found.

Saturday, December 23

It's another cold day, but we decided to be brave and go out because Papa was going to take us shopping.

We took a bus near our house to Flatbush Avenue, which gave us a chance to see more of Brooklyn without being too cold. I kept my face glued to the window, watching the streets go by: more row houses, lines of detached ones, too, and then clusters of giant buildings that could house most of Port-au-Prince.

Moy pointed out the parks, which were empty, the

trees bared by the cold. None of Granmè Melina and Granpè Nozial's mango, almond, and avocado trees would survive here in the cold.

Manman called our attention to churches, beauty parlors, and restaurants, all of them bigger than any buildings I had ever seen in Port-au-Prince. I could tell that these buildings amazed her, too, by their size and matching constructions, by the fact that there appeared to be so few people in them, compared to how crowded they would have been in Port-au-Prince.

Moy said the names of the mechanics' shops and gas stations out loud as Papa corrected his pronunciation in English. The signs here were not as colorful as the ones that Bòs Dezi made or as brightly embellished as the ones in Carrefour, but some were written in lights, which impressed Moy nonetheless.

I wish Thérèse could see all of this. She would be so amazed. Having spent even less time in Port-au-Prince than I have, Brooklyn would have been all the more startling to her.

Looking around, I kept thinking the same thing I did the first time I went to Port-au-Prince with Manman. How can some people live in a small village in the mountains with only lamps for illumination at night and others live in a city where every street corner has its own giant lamp? It made the world seem unbalanced somehow.

Flatbush Avenue was so crowded we almost had to walk in the middle of the street. The street felt like a city unto itself, like the market in downtown Port-au-Prince, where every step brings you face-to-face with someone else.

Flatbush Avenue was a kind of market, too, except the vendors were inside and not out on the street. The stores were decorated with Christmas lights and people seemed to be buying everything off the shelves.

If she were here on Flatbush Avenue, Madame Auguste would have bought a gift for everyone in our class. I wish I could buy a present for everyone in our class. I know that Pouchon would have liked the electric train set. Thérèse would have liked a sewing machine, which looked too big to be a toy. I kept thinking of all the students in my class and what toys they would have liked until I made a game of it, while winding talking dolls, watching train sets go around sharp bends on narrow tracks, and listening to sirens on small police cars left out to tempt buyers.

When everyone, including Moy, had gathered quite

a few packages, Papa asked me what kind of present we should get for Tante Rose. I thought of the perfect gift. We went to a small photo studio owned by a Haitian man on Flatbush Avenue and took a family photo that we would not only send to Tante Rose but to Granmè and Granpè Nozial as well.

Sunday, December 24

Franck invited us to go to Christmas Eve Mass with him at Saint Jerome's. The mass was in Creole. There were so many Haitians in the church that if not for the cold, I would have thought we were at a mass with Tante Rose in Port-au-Prince.

I thought of Thérèse playing the part of Mary in the Nativity play in Beau Jour. The whole village would gather to watch the play.

For many of the parents, this would be one of the few moments when they would see their children's book learning at work. I think this is one of the reasons Madame Auguste held the pageant in the first place — Madame Auguste who, like Tante Rose, had lived in Beau Jour as a child and had gone to the city for schooling, but had returned to open the school because she was the first person in her family to have learned to read and write.

At Saint Jerome's, Haiti did not seem so far away. I felt that if I reached out and touched anyone at the mass, I could be back in Haiti again, as though every person there was carrying a piece of Haiti with them in the warmth of their skin, beneath their winter coats.

Later

Before we went to sleep, Moy surprised us by bringing out his *tap tap fanal*. He had undone it in Beau Jour and put it with his clothes and reconstructed it again last night, keeping it hidden until now.

Papa had not seen a *fanal* in a long time. Moy hung the *fanal* from the kitchen entrance like a plant. We all looked up at it as though it was the star of Bethlehem.

Monday, December 25

The first thing we did when we got up this morning was call Tante Rose to wish her *Jwaye Nowèl*.

I asked her how things were in the capital. She said it was calm again. At least there were no more bombings.

I helped Manman make breakfast and then it was time to open our presents.

Papa gave me the typewriter I had asked him to send me after I had seen a secretary using one at the money-transfer place in Léogâne.

I immediately started tapping at the keys, making a *click-clack* melody with them.

Slipping a blank page into the typewriter, I typed my first note in English.

Dear Papa,

Thank you.

Tuesday, December 26

Manman and Papa had their first fight in New York. I could hear them arguing all the way from my room.

Manman had turned up the stove too high and burnt some rice she was cooking.

"You are not cooking on sticks and rocks anymore," Papa said. "You can control *this* fire."

"Oh!" Manman said. "Are you calling me a peasant? Don't forget, we both come from the same place. The sticks and rocks were fine for you before."

"I'm just saying you don't have to turn it up all the way," Papa said.

"Don't look down your nose at old rags," Manman said, using one of her proverbs. "Remember, they fit you fine before."

Wednesday, December 27

I used my typewriter to write my first letter to Thérèse, telling her about all the new things I had seen and done: Flatbush Avenue, the shops, Christmas Eve Mass. I told her how much I missed her and how I wish she could be here to share these things with me.

Moy had some letters of his own to mail to Bòs Dezi and his other friends in Léogâne. Papa, Moy, and I walked to the post office to send the letters off.

Thursday, December 28

Papa showed us how to find a Haitian station on the kitchen radio. The station we found was just like the ones in Haiti, with music and news programs in Creole, and discussion programs where people called in to debate different topics.

Some people called in about the American presidential election, which had also taken place this past November. Apparently the votes had been so close that the two candidates had taken the matter all the way to the United States Supreme Court.

The caller said how similar this was to elections in Haiti, where the results were often in question.

Friday, December 29

We heard on the Haitian radio station that there would be a big snowstorm tomorrow, so Papa took us shopping for the ingredients for our New Year's Day *soup joumou*, squash soup.

We went to a shop on Nostrand Avenue, where Papa buys ingredients for the food cooked in Franck's restaurants and chose our beautiful squash, which we were told came directly from Haiti.

Saturday, December 30

When we woke up, it was snowing. It continued to snow all day. Moy and Papa went out now and then to clear the path in front of our door, but it was useless. More snow kept falling, burying the cars out front.

I find the snow less beautiful now, messy even. When so much of it is falling, it looks like it can be dangerous, like it could cave in the roof above our heads.

Sunday, December 31

Papa took us to a Laundromat to wash our clothes and the house linen in a machine so we wouldn't carry the dirt of an old year into a new one.

What an indulgence not to have to wash our clothes by hand! This was a great relief because I worried about washing my new heavy clothes myself.

In the afternoon, we made our *soup joumou*. The house smelled like Granmè Melina's cooking shed on New Year's Eve.

Monday, January 1, 2001

It's a new year in our new life. As we sat around the kitchen table, each one of us quietly enjoying our soup, I thought of the different meanings of the day. Of course it is the start of a whole new period, but it is also a great anniversary for us Haitians — Haitian Independence Day. A hundred and ninety seven years ago, our ancestors had declared our small island a free nation.

Later

Papa will return to work tomorrow, and Moy and I will be starting school.

Papa said that I would be in a special class for students just like me, who had recently come from Haiti and did not yet speak English. The lessons would be in Creole.

Moy will start English classes at Saint Jerome's. (This is where Papa had learned English after he had just arrived.) When Moy knows enough English, he will take a test. If he passes it, he can go to university.

Tuesday, January 2

I woke up early, extremely nervous about my first day at school. Papa had already purchased my school supplies, pens and pencils, notebooks, and a backpack to carry them in.

As we ate our morning meal, Papa showed me the bus route on a map for my return trip home. Franck is letting him drive one of the restaurant's vans to and from work. He will use the van to drop me off at school, but I will have to find my way home by myself. (Papa assures me that it is very easy.)

I think it is Moy who has it easy. He'll be going to afternoon classes and he doesn't even have to take a bus.

Later

The school is in a gray concrete building, facing a slew of giant housing complexes, which Papa said are called "projects." The projects are so tall that they look like mountains with windows.

We went directly to the main office, where teachers and school administrators were sitting behind desks, performing different tasks to prepare for the school day. Papa stood quietly facing the desks, waiting for one of the administrators to look up. Finally, a man walked over to us.

Papa's English was not nearly as fluid as the man's was. Still, Papa managed to explain why we were there. In his quick-fire speech, the man asked about my vaccination and medical papers. ("Vaccination" and "medical" are similar words in Creole as in English.) When Papa handed him the papers, the man walked back to his desk and picked up a form. He filled in some of the form, then gave Papa the rest to finish.

The man called someone else over, an older woman. The woman looked down at the form and told us in Creole that I had been assigned to Class 8M5. Papa asked what room that was. She said she would take us.

My knees were shaking as we followed the woman through the hallway. At times, I fell behind Papa and the woman, my new backpack weighing me down.

There was a long buzz and suddenly it was mayhem, with students pouring into the halls, some running and knocking into one another as they climbed the staircase around us.

My main room, the homeroom, was on the fourth floor in a corner near the stairwell. The students were beginning to arrive, slipping into their seats as we approached the teacher's desk. The woman from the main office introduced the homeroom teacher as Mr. Marius.

Mr. Marius was a young man, looking not much more mature than many of his students. The woman from the main office gave him my records. He looked them over, then said, "Bienvenue, Celiane."

The class was full now and everyone was looking at me. While the lady from the main office was leaving, I tried to keep my back to the other students and concentrate on Mr. Marius.

Papa was telling him (too loudly for my taste) what a good student I had been in Beau Jour, how my teacher had always "appreciated" me, how I had often been first in my class.

I kept wishing Papa wasn't saying those things. From the silence in the room, I could tell the others were listening, adding Papa's words to their first impressions of me.

I had already decided that I was no longer going to try to outshine everyone in class and Papa was ruining my plans. Being the teacher's favorite was no way to make friends.

When it was time for Papa to leave, he handed me a piece of paper with his telephone number at work, our home address, two quarters, and a five-dollar bill for me to take a taxi if I got lost. He told me (again too loudly) that I should not be afraid to call him at work if I needed him. Some of the students were smiling when I waved good-bye to Papa, who looked back one last time before the door closed behind him. I wanted so badly to go with Papa, but I knew this was not possible, so I turned back to the classroom and tried to find a desk.

"You are there, Celiane," Mr. Marius said, pointing to an empty desk in the back of the room. Mr. Marius had a chart of small cards lined up in front of him. He explained that this seat would be mine for the rest of the school year, as he handed me a blank card on which to write my name. When I was done, he placed the card on the chart to match where I was sitting.

"Celiane," he said. "We have a presentation we make whenever someone new comes to us. Class, let us begin."

Each of the students took turns getting up to tell

me his or her name and something about the school. The first boy who spoke reminded me of Pouchon. He looked just as serious as Pouchon, too, wearing a crisp white shirt buttoned up all the way to the top.

"My name is Faidherbe," he said. "You are now a student at Jackie Robinson Intermediate School."

A boy named Gary, with a blue bandanna around his head, explained that Jackie Robinson was the first African-American baseball player in something called the major leagues.

Once Gary was done talking, Mr. Marius asked him to remove his bandanna, which Mr. Marius said was a gang symbol. Gary denied that his bandanna was a gang symbol, but took it off anyway.

The next row told me things like where the bathroom and water fountains were, and the best times to go to avoid some of the more quarrelsome kids who liked to tease the Haitian students.

I learned from the third row that the school day was divided into something called "periods" and that we would all be together for six periods — the different teachers would come to us in this room — except for gym class, where we had to do some kind of physical exercise in the gymnasium with students from the rest of the school, and "lunch period," where we would receive a free meal. (Mr. Marius handed me a book of numbered tickets for the free meals at that point.)

At the end of the presentations, Mr. Marius added that I should not worry about feeling lost at first, that slowly I would get used to my surroundings.

"It was the same for everyone here at first," he said. "Right class?"

The class reluctantly answered, "Yes," as if he were forcing them to remember a time they would rather forget.

Later

At the beginning of every class period, there was at least five minutes devoted to me. I had to introduce myself to each teacher and fill out a card and receive a book related to the subject.

The subjects ranged from science to American history, mathematics to art, which Moy would have liked. However, the subject we spent the most time on was English.

The periods themselves went by quickly. The forty

or so minutes were too brief for me to fully grasp more than a few points in the lesson, even though they were in Creole.

Later

The lunch period was chaotic, with students rushing in from everywhere to wait in line. I kept getting pushed to the back of the line by students who could obviously tell I would not complain.

When I finally got my lunch, I had to eat it quickly, at a corner table already abandoned by a group that had eaten and moved to another table to chat with friends.

Later

In afternoon homeroom, Mr. Marius asked about my day. It was not nearly as frightening as I'd expected, I told him, even though I really didn't know what I had been expecting.

The bell rang and the way everyone ran out of the school, you would think there was a flood or a fire.

Later

I walked around for what felt like a thousand years, looking for the bus. I went down one street, which then led to another and another. Every building, large and small, looked the same to me, from the corner stores with their shutters raised, to the supermarkets with spaces for cars out front.

Every face that passed me seemed distant, and even if people were willing to help me, I would not have known how to ask for help.

It was cold and my feet were beginning to feel numb. I felt like Galipòt, looking for his fourth leg. I understand now what Manman meant when she talked about being lost in the city. I felt as though I was looking both for my new home as well as for myself.

After all, who was I, here without my family, without the father who had sent for me and the mother and brother I had come with?

I was trying to find the school where I had started out. I was sure once I got there, things would seem better.

I had made no friends at school. I know this should not be a surprise on the first day, but I had hoped that someone would volunteer to look after me, show me — not just tell me — where things were and what to do. This is what I would have done if a new pupil had arrived from New York at the school in Beau Jour.

As I walked down yet another street, I began to blame Papa. Why had he left it up to me to find my way home? On my first day at that? Maybe he didn't love me after all.

It was getting dark. I was shivering. I had been walking for so long I couldn't tell what time it was. Some of the blocks I walked up and down were desolate. Others were filled with people walking home. Some of the buildings had barred windows, through which I could see people cooking and watching television. I wanted so badly to be inside, anywhere inside, where it was warm.

I thought of the money Papa had given me to take a taxi in case I got lost. How was I to find a taxi? Papa had not shown me how to identify the taxis. Would the word *taxi* be written in bold letters on the side of the cars?

I remembered Moy holding out his hand for taxis in Port-au-Prince and I held out mine, too. As I stood there with my arm extended, people stopped to look me over, then continued on their way. Maybe I looked too young to be calling a taxi. Perhaps you had to be an adult to be in a taxi here. I am not sure a taxi would have stopped for me in Port-au-Prince, either.

Finally, a black car stopped. The driver rolled down the window and asked me something in English. I handed the driver the piece of paper Papa had given me. The driver said something that sounded like a command, which I did not understand. He repeated it a few times, his voice growing louder each time.

I did not move. The driver got impatient, handed me back the paper and drove away.

On the paper, along with our address, Papa had written his telephone number at work. I would need to find a telephone. Why hadn't Papa shown me how to use the public telephone?

A woman walked past slowly, staring at me. At first she went by like all the others, but then took a few steps back until she was standing right next to me.

She asked me a question in which I recognized the word "problem." I yelled out, "Telephone," a few times until she pointed at a public telephone across the street.

I waited until the light was green and walked across to the telephone. The woman followed me there. I lifted the receiver and dialed the telephone number on the paper. I heard a cold voice, like a machine speaking, and hung up.

The woman took the piece of paper from me, removed some coins out of her own pocket, dialed the number, then handed me the headset.

The phone rang and rang, but no one answered. Papa was probably home, or on his way there. I did not know the telephone number at home. Papa had not written it down, probably figuring that neither Moy nor Manman, who were at home, would be able to help me if I got lost.

I was back where I'd started.

The woman looked down at me, perplexed. I said the word *taxi* and pointed to the address on the paper.

She walked me to the street corner and held out her hand until another car stopped. She and the driver exchanged a few words, then she read the address out to him from the paper.

She looked back at me to confirm the address after she read it, then she paid the driver with money from her own pocket. I tried to offer her the money Papa had given me, but she shook her head and said, "No."

She opened the door and waited for me to get in the car.

I said, "Thank you," and slipped inside.

She closed the door, and slowly the driver pulled away.

As I looked back, she was still standing in the corner, watching us drive away. The driver took a turn and she disappeared from my sight. I pushed myself back in the backseat, grateful that I had run into her.

The driver was talking to me, but I understood nothing he was saying. He gave up and kept driving.

I soon found myself on a familiar street, on the block where we live. I let out a shriek of recognition when I saw our house. I thanked the driver and ran to our front door.

Manman looked worried when she came to the door with Moy beside her. Hadn't school let out long ago? she asked.

"I was lost," I said.

Papa was still not home from work.

"We have to talk to Papa about doing this differently," she said, "so you don't get lost again."

Later

When Papa came home I told him what happened. He said he was sorry he had not made better arrangements for me to get home, but he appeared a little angry and disappointed in me, too.

It wasn't anything he said, just the way his face looked, tightly drawn and strained. Perhaps we, especially me, were going to be more of a burden to him than he had first thought.

Wednesday, January 3

Papa drove me to school and picked me up. He said he would do that every day now, until I felt I could take the bus home by myself. This meant some adjustment in his afternoon work schedule and I felt bad for that.

Thursday, January 4

I still don't have one person to talk to at school. None of the students have approached me and I am too shy to approach them.

Friday, January 5

Tonight while I was sitting at the kitchen table trying to understand my homework, Moy walked over and gave me a gentle tap on the head like he used to in Beau Jour.

"How are you getting along?" he asked.

I told him I was not doing so well. I was having trouble with the lessons and I didn't have any friends.

"Tell anyone who makes friends with you," he said, "that your brother is a very good painter and if they become your friend, he will paint portraits of them, their mothers, their fathers, their brothers, their sisters, their uncles, their aunts, their grandparents, their godparents . . ."

He listed every possible family connection until we were both laughing too hard for him to continue.

Sunday, January 7

At Moy's suggestion, I spent the whole weekend reviewing everything we have studied in class since I started school. I think if I review the week's lessons thoroughly every weekend, I might be able to keep up.

Handsome and clever, too, that's Moy.

Monday, January 8

Manman started work today in one of Franck's restaurants, the same one where Papa works. She will be cooking in the kitchen. She seemed happy to leave the house, even if the work is only part-time for now.

She will be home by the time I return from school every day.

Tuesday, January 9

Manman likes her work. I am so glad. I just hope she can control the stove at the restaurant. She still has trouble controlling the one we have at home.

Wednesday, January 10

Moy has taken up running. Every morning, he gets up, puts on his exercise clothes, and goes running in the cold.

Thursday, January 11

Mr. Marius put me together with someone today. (I think he felt sorry for me.) She is Immacula Cadet, a soft-spoken girl, whose best friend is Faidherbe, the boy who always wears his shirts buttoned up to the top. Immacula wears only black clothes, as though she is mourning the death of a loved one.

After the morning homeroom, Mr. Marius called us both outside and said he noticed from our address cards that we lived in the same neighborhood and that perhaps we should take the bus together.

Immacula asked how come she hadn't seen me at the bus stop in the afternoons. I said my father picked me up after school and dropped me off in the morning, but I wanted to learn to take the bus by myself.

Mr. Marius asked if she could help me do that and she said yes.

Friday, January 12

I told Papa I found someone to help me with the bus and would like to try it again. He said if I really wanted to, I could.

Papa will still take me in the mornings on his way to work, but starting next week, I will come home on the bus with Faidherbe and Immacula.

Saturday, January 13

Moy is painting again. When he paints inside the house, however, the smell makes our eyes water, so even though it's cold outside, he has to open all of the windows.

Sunday, January 14

The weekend lesson review is a great success. I am starting to make a little more sense of my classes.

Monday, January 15

No school today. Our American History teacher, Mr. Casimir, had told us that it is Martin Luther King, Jr.'s birthday.

Martin Luther King, Jr., he told us, was a man who dedicated his life to fighting for the rights of black people in America. Even though we were not born here, he said, it is thanks to the efforts of Martin Luther King, Jr. and others like him, that we are able to go anywhere we want, shop in any store, and go to any school.

I am going to make it a point to learn more about Martin Luther King, Jr.

Tuesday, January 16

Immacula didn't come to school today. Faidherbe came up to me and told me that Immacula had called him on the telephone yesterday and had asked him to take the bus with me.

Later

I took the bus home with Faidherbe. It was even more crowded than a *tap tap* in Léogâne, completely packed with kids from our school and another school nearby.

Faidherbe and I somehow found a pole to hold. Each time the bus stopped, which was often, we were pulled forward, pounding into someone else.

I was happy when my turn came to get off. I left Faidherbe to continue his ride. The bus stop is around the corner from our house, too close for me to get lost.

Wednesday, January 17

Immacula is back. She did not volunteer anything about her absence yesterday. However, at lunchtime, even though I was not trying to listen, I overheard her and Faidherbe talking about Immacula's mother, who, it seems, spends a lot of time working as a home attendant for other people and very little time at her own home, which leaves only Immacula to take care of her younger sisters.

Thursday, January 18

Tonight after supper, Papa made us sit around the radio to listen to the farewell speech of the outgoing president of the United States, President William Jefferson Clinton. (This reminded me of listening to election reports on Tante Rose's radio in Haiti.)

The speech was simultaneously translated into Creole by a broadcaster on the Haitian radio station. The words I remember most are:

> In our hearts and in our laws, we must treat all our people with fairness and dignity . . . regardless of when they arrived in our country.

I felt as though he was talking about Manman, Papa, Moy, and me.

Friday, January 19

When I woke up this morning, I heard music coming from the kitchen radio. The radio was louder than usual. From the kitchen doorway, I saw Manman and Papa in each other's arms, dancing. They both seemed embarrassed when they saw me watching. I wish Moy could have seen this, too, but he was out on an early morning run.

Saturday, January 20

We listened to the inaugural address of President George W. Bush, the forty-third president of the United States. It was also translated into Creole by a Haitian broadcaster.

Again, I picked out my favorite part:

America has never been united by blood or birth or soil. We are bound by ideals that move us beyond our backgrounds, lift us above interests and teach us what it means to be citizens. Every child must be taught these principles. Every citizen must uphold them. And every immigrant, by embracing these ideals makes our country more, not less, American.

Monday, January 22

Mr. Casimir discussed President Bush's speech in class. I was pleased he chose to talk about the same part of the speech that had stood out for me.

This led to a discussion about what Haitians have contributed to this country.

I was surprised to learn that a man who was born in Saint-Marc, Haiti, Jean Baptiste Point du Sable, was the first settler in an American city called Chicago. I also learned that a great naturalist, John James Audubon, was born in Les Cayes, Haiti, on April 26, 1785.

As a French colony, Haiti did a lot of commercial trade with the United States. Haitian volunteers fought along with Americans in the Siege of Savannah during the American Revolutionary War. One of the volunteers was Henri Christophe, who later became king of Haiti.

Tuesday, January 23

I went to the library and made a copy of one of Mr. Audubon's drawings for Moy. It is a painting of a beautiful bright-red flamingo. Perched on the edge of a sea cliff, Mr. Audubon's flamingo looked as though it could have been painted on a *tap tap*.

Wednesday, January 24

As we waited for the bus together this afternoon, Immacula and Faidherbe tried to outdo one another with scary stories about the school, which they wanted to share with me, they said, as cautionary tales.

This was another version of Mr. Marius's welcome presentation, they said, the real thing.

Immacula told me how some of the kids at school were in gangs which were differentiated by colors.

Faidherbe told me that it was best to avoid wearing

either red or blue so I would not be mistaken for a member of either the Bloods or the Crips gangs.

Immacula told me how two years ago, after a night basketball game, a student from our school had stabbed a player from another team who died on the way to the hospital. Faidherbe said that was why his family did not let him take part in any afterschool activities.

Thursday, January 25

I finally got a letter from Thérèse. She had not yet received mine, but had gotten my address from Tante Rose so she could write to me. She promised to write again, but did not put a return address.

Thérèse's mother, like many poor mothers in the provinces, has decided to send her to live with a family of a man her mother sometimes sells vetiver to in the market in Léogâne. The man's family lives in the capital and he has taken Thérèse to work at his house, promising to send her to a better school than Madame Auguste's.

This doesn't sound good. Most girls who end up in this kind of arrangement never go to school. They work from morning to night, waiting on the families, cooking and cleaning, and the families rarely spend money on their education.

Tante Rose was involved in this same kind of arrangement when she was my age. My grandparents — Tante Rose and Papa's parents, the ones she had lit the candle for on All Saints' Day — had sent her to the capital to work for a family of a coffee speculator her mother had met in the market in Léogâne. The coffee speculator had promised to send Tante Rose to school in exchange for Tante Rose's working at her house, but she never did.

She and her husband threw Tante Rose out of their house when their son, who was ten years older than Tante Rose, attacked Tante Rose and she complained to them.

Tante Rose was too ashamed to return home, so she went to an orphanage and offered her services there. She worked for school fees and that's how she got her education.

Tante Rose was very lucky. Perhaps Thérèse will be, too. But for every story like Tante Rose's, there are thousands of girls who end up alone in the city with nothing.

Friday, January 26

I am starting to understand my lessons a lot better now. I even got an 82 percent on an English spelling test. I had memorized those words as though they were pictures and reproduced them on the page exactly the way I saw them in my head.

Immacula, Faidherbe, and I now study together during our lunch hour and this helps me a lot. I write a list of questions and whatever I don't understand, they explain to me.

Saturday, January 27

Manman brought home some food from work. She seems to like her job a lot, most of all because she doesn't have to cook at home in the evenings anymore. Most of what we eat now is leftover food from the restaurant. It feels strange to be sharing Manman's cooking with so many people. Those people are lucky to have Manman cook for them.

Sunday, January 28

Moy practiced some of his English on me today.

"How are you, Celiane Espérance?" he asked.

I said, *"I am fine, thank you."*

We giggled through the whole thing.

In Beau Jour, when I used to think about coming to New York, I had imagined that speaking in another language would make me a different person. But here Moy and I were, saying a few words to each other in English, and we were still the same people we have always been, the same people living in a different language.

Monday, January 29

A fight broke out outside the school. Faidherbe, Immacula, and I were making our way to the edge of the crowd when a gun went off.

The students quickly scattered in all directions. Immacula grabbed me by the arm and the three of us started running to the bus stop.

I was relieved when we got on the bus. Immacula asked if we would come over to her apartment for a while. After hearing that gun go off, she was very frightened.

Thinking of the gunfire I'd heard nightly from Tante Rose's house during the election period, so was I.

Later

A school bus dropped Immacula's three younger sisters off soon after we arrived at her apartment. The oldest of the girls was eight years old, the middle one, seven, and the youngest, six. Not having sisters myself, I found Immacula's adorable, like little dolls.

Immacula's living-room wall was covered with pictures of her mother and father and three sisters. There was only one picture of Immacula with the rest of her family.

When she saw me looking at the pictures, Immacula walked over and explained that she was hardly in any of the family photos because her parents had left her in Haiti with relatives while they settled here. Like Papa, they had overstayed tourist visas and it took them nine years to get the proper papers and send for Immacula.

In the meantime, Immacula's three sisters were born here, in America. She didn't meet them until eight months ago, two months before her father died.

Imagine waiting that long to see your father, only to have him die two months after you arrive.

Faidherbe had an interesting story as well. His aunt and uncle, whom he is living with here in Brooklyn, had had to adopt him in order to send for him. His parents were still living in Haiti. He couldn't wait to get older and make lots of money to bring them here.

The three of us started on our homework and it wasn't until it was dark that I realized maybe I should have telephoned Manman — I now carried the house number everywhere with me — to let her know where I was.

Manman was furious. Even Papa was already home, she said. Papa asked where I was when he got on the phone. He sounded angry, too.

"First, Moy and now you," Papa said.

"What did Moy do?" I asked.

"Tell me where you are and I'll come for you," he said.

While I was gathering my things to go outside and wait for Papa, Immacula's landlord came knocking on the door. Following Immacula's orders, Faidherbe and

I hid in the corner and listened as the landlord questioned Immacula.

Faidherbe explained, in whispers, that the landlord was asking if Immacula's mother was home. When he found out that she was not, he said he wanted to speak to Immacula's mother as soon as possible. After the landlord left, I went out and waited for Papa outside Immacula's apartment building. When he pulled up in the van, he pushed the door open and said nothing.

"I am sorry, Papa," I said as I got in. "I did not intend to worry you."

I wanted to tell him about my day, about the fight at school, but he was looking very tired and angry, too.

During the ride home, he seemed as far away from me as he had been during those five years we'd been apart. And I felt as unable to speak to him as I had been when Manman had put the cassette player in front of me and had asked me to say more than a greeting to him.

When we were close to the house, he finally blurted out, "I worked every waking moment for five years to get you, your mother, and brother here. Do you know that?"

"Yes, Papa," I said.

"Is this how you show your gratitude?"

"I am sorry, Papa. It was just that —"

"The money I sent you every month did not simply appear out of the air," he said, interrupting me. "I worked all the time. I am still working all the time. If I didn't work in a restaurant, I never would have seen the inside of one. I never went dancing, never went on a vacation. All you could do, the three of you, is give me some peace. I have earned it."

Papa's words reminded me of the ending of Granpè Nozial's ice story. Even if Granpè Nozial's ice man, who had spent so many years telling his friends about ice, had been able to bring a block of it up to the mountain, his friends would have been let down by the ice. Having tried and failed many times to bring the ice to his friends, Granpè Nozial's ice man would have probably described it in such glorious detail that his friends would have constructed a block of crystal or diamonds in their minds. Finally, if he had succeeded in bringing the real thing to them, they probably would have looked at it with some disappointment, examining its frailness, its fragility, and asking, "Is that all it is?"

Perhaps Papa was feeling the same about us, just as I was feeling about him. After five years of fantasies, visions, and dreams, we were all bound to be a little disappointed in one another.

Later

It seems Moy only went to English class the first week he was enrolled, then quit. Papa found this out when he stopped by Saint Jerome's.

Manman and Papa put Moy and me together for a joint scolding.

I was the first to be given the opportunity to explain myself.

"Celiane, where were you?" Manman asked.

I explained that I had gone to the apartment of a girl from school.

"Celiane, no more going off to strangers' apartments, people we don't know," Papa said, interrupting me again. "We must know where you are so we know where to look for you if something happens."

"Yes, Papa," I said.

Papa seemed anxious to get to Moy's situation. Moy had a lot more to explain.

Why hadn't he continued his classes?

Moy said he would eventually re-enroll. But for the next few weeks he wanted to finish a series of paintings.

"What is two hours a day to learn English if you have the rest of your life to paint?" Manman asked.

"What about tailoring?" Papa asked. "Making clothes?"

Moy declared he was no longer interested in that. All he wanted to do was paint.

Papa announced that from now on Moy would be forbidden to paint.

"*Ki sa?*" Moy shouted. "What?"

He was getting ready to make a case for himself, but Papa did not give him a chance.

"Moy, you go to your classes or you go back to Haiti," Papa said.

Papa then went to his room and slammed the door behind him. Manman followed him there. Soon after, Moy and I could hear them arguing.

"Don't threaten him like that," Manman said.

"I can't let him sit around and waste his life," Papa said.

"Maybe we can make an exchange with him," Manman said. "If he takes his English classes, he can go to school to study painting, the way he was studying to be a tailor."

"Study painting? What good would that do him?"

"It is what he has always done," Manman said. "It is the only thing that seems to make his heart happy."

"It takes more than a happy heart to eat and have a roof over your head in this country," Papa said. "If anything it takes a lot of unhappiness to do that."

Moy couldn't take any more. He changed into his running clothes and left.

Tuesday, January 30

In homeroom, Immacula said she was sorry for getting me in trouble with my parents. I told her it was not her fault; it was mine for not calling and letting them know where I was.

While I was talking to Immacula, I kept thinking of Thérèse and how Thérèse would have been as interested in Moy's situation as mine. Immacula didn't even know Moy and it would take too much explaining to tell her Moy's story, ending with what happened last night.

Aside from Immacula and Faidherbe, all the other students were talking about the fight and shooting. A few of the kids said that one of Gary's gang friends had fired the gun. Thank goodness the boy who had been shot was not killed.

Gary was sitting quietly at his desk, reading a comic book, pretending not to hear the conversations. He was not wearing his usual blue bandana. In fact, he was dressed like Faidbherbe, in a yellow shirt and navy slacks, as though his mother had picked out his clothes for him that morning.

During all the talk about the shooting, I could not get my mind off Moy. I was worried about Papa carrying out his threat and sending him back to Haiti, or that Moy, angry with Papa for forbidding him to paint, would volunteer to go back to live with Tante Rose, splitting us up again.

Wednesday, January 31

I still have not given Moy the Audubon photocopy. Since he cannot paint anymore, it probably would make him sad.

Thursday, February 1

Manman had a chat with Moy before Papa came home from work. She begged him to go back to his classes in order to keep the peace with Papa, and to remain with us in New York.

She said she had spoken to Papa and everything would be all right if Moy stopped painting for a while and went back to his classes.

Moy agreed to go back to his classes, not because of Papa's threat, I think, but because he adores Manman and he sees how sad this conflict with Papa is making her.

Friday, February 2

Moy and Papa are still not talking. They only nod hello to each other, once in the morning and then again at night before they go to bed. Whenever Moy is in the house, he walks around with a big frown on his face, one just like Papa's.

Saturday, February 3

This afternoon I noticed fresh paint on Moy's running shoes. I have a suspicion that he is painting somewhere else.

Sunday, February 4

Franck called to say that even though it was Manman and Papa's day off, he needed them to work.

As soon as Manman and Papa left, Moy got dressed and gathered his things to go out.

"Where are you going?" I asked.

"Running," he said.

"With your bag?" I said, pointing to the backpack in his hand.

He paused, as if to judge whether or not I could be trusted.

"Should I tell you?" he asked, thinking it over.

"I won't tell Manman and Papa," I said.

"There is a girl in my class," he says. "She has her own apartment. She is letting me paint there."

"Is she your girlfriend?" I asked.

"I am wasting time," he said. "I need to go."

"Wait, I have something for you," I said.

I ran to my room and found the Audubon photocopy. He looked it over and handed it back to me.

"Put it on your wall," he said. "This house needs some decoration."

And then he left.

Later

Papa came home with a small bandage on his forehead. He had been in a car accident, ramming the restaurant van into the back of another car. He was not too badly hurt. He only got a small cut from hitting his head on the steering wheel when he struck the other car, but he looked so shaken he could barely talk.

"The road was *glise*, slippery," Manman explained. "He tried to stop the van, but it wouldn't stop."

Manman had been in the van with him, but she was all right.

When Papa finally spoke it was to ask where Moy was.

I told him Moy had gone out.

"Out where?" he asked.

"Probably running again," Manman said.

"So late?" Papa asked, looking at the clock on the living-room wall. It was almost midnight.

"I'm sure he'll be back soon," Manman said.

We all sat down in the living room to wait for Moy's return.

Monday, February 5

Moy did not come back until about 6:00 A.M. this morning. Papa must have carried me to bed because I woke up in my room to the sound of Moy and Papa yelling at one another.

I walked out to the living room to see Papa and Moy with their faces within inches of each other's. They looked like they were going to get into one of those fights that Moy had been in so often in Léogâne.

Manman was standing between them, trying to keep them apart.

"Where were you?" Papa was shouting.

"I didn't know I was coming to prison here," Moy shouted back.

"If you're too grown to live here, then get out!" Papa said.

It was then that Moy must have finally noticed the small bandage on Papa's forehead.

"What happened to your head?" he asked Papa.

"If you cared what happened to any of us," Papa said, "you would have been here at home with your sister."

"Victor," Manman said. "Please lower your voice." Then turning to Moy, she whispered, "Your father hit a car with the van. It's a small cut."

Moy walked over to the couch, sat down, and buried his face in his hands. I could tell he was feeling bad for what happened to Papa and even worse that he hadn't been here all night.

Papa turned away from both Manman and Moy and walked to the kitchen.

A few minutes later, I followed him there and found him sitting at the table with his face lowered against the edge of the table. When he heard my footsteps, he raised his head. He was crying.

I walked over and put my hand on his shoulder. I

thought he would push it away, but he just let it rest there for a while until he stopped crying.

Then he got up, went back to the living room, and told Moy to leave the house immediately, go back to wherever he had spent the night.

Manman begged Moy not to leave, but Moy picked up his bag and walked out.

Later

I spent the whole day at school thinking about Moy. I hope he is safe wherever he is. He is probably with that girl, the girl at whose house he has been painting. I hope he is okay.

Tuesday, February 6

Papa did not leave the house today. I took the bus to school by myself.

No word from Moy.

Later

Franck came by tonight to see how Papa is doing. Franck said the repairs on the van wouldn't be too expensive and he would pay for them.

Papa insisted that he wanted to pay for the repairs himself since the accident was his fault. He was probably feeling ashamed that Franck was always taking care of things for him.

Wednesday, February 7

Tonight we listened to a report of President Aristide's inauguration on the radio. The reporter said that before President Aristide spoke, two white doves, which had been released by school children, stopped and rested on the podium for a while.

I would like to think that those doves represent the seven-year-old girl and teenage boy who had died before the elections last November, their spirits returning to express hope for a more peaceful Haiti.

In his speech President Aristide said, "Honor and respect and bravo for the Tenth department Haitians living abroad. There is no place like home."

Papa and Manman listened to the speech closely.

They both looked pensive, as if imagining themselves in the crowd outside of the national palace in Port-au-Prince.

"After two hundred years of political violence," President Aristide said, "there is only one road that will lead to complete deliverance. This is the road of peace."

Thursday, February 8

We called Tante Rose this morning to see how she is doing. After the inauguration, she is cautiously hopeful, she said.

Papa did not tell her about Moy, that he had left the house and that we didn't even know where he was.

Later

Still not a word from Moy. Manman is getting more and more nervous about him and even though he doesn't say it I think Papa is, too.

Oh Moy, where are you?

Friday, February 9

During homeroom, a police woman came into our classroom and took Gary away. Mr. Marius followed them outside and when he came back, he told us that Gary was not being arrested, but was among many kids in the school who were going to be questioned about the shooting.

Saturday, February 10

Still no word from Moy.

Will we ever see him again?

Sunday, February 11

Manman and Papa are barely speaking to each other. I suppose the most important thing they could talk about is Moy and that's become too painful a subject.

I blame Papa for driving Moy away. I blame Manman for not doing more to stop Moy from leaving. I blame Moy for leaving. I blame myself — I am not sure why I blame myself, but I do anyway.

Monday, February 12

There is no school today. According to Mr. Casimir, today is the birthday of Abraham Lincoln, the sixteenth president of the United States.

After Haiti gained its independence in 1804, the United States refused to acknowledge Haiti, because it was thought that a free black republic would encourage American slaves to revolt against their masters.

According to Mr. Casimir, it was Lincoln who sent the first United States ambassador to Haiti in 1862. Later he picked Frederick Douglass, a black American, to be his representative there.

I am filling my head with all this information in order to forget for a few minutes that it's been seven days since we have seen or heard from Moy.

Tuesday, February 13

Gary is back. It seems that he was not involved in the shooting after all.

Later

Still no word from Moy. Papa went to Saint Jerome's to see if Moy had gone to his classes there. He hadn't.

I wish Moy had told me the name of the girl who was letting him paint in her apartment. Maybe Papa could have found out where she lives.

Wednesday, February 14

Papa brought Manman a bouquet of roses because it is Saint Valentine's Day. At school some of the girls wore red. Even Immacula wore a red scarf with her black dress.

Thursday, February 15

Moy came by tonight right before we went to bed. I was so happy to see him again. His sneakers were covered with paint and he looked a little thinner, but otherwise he seemed fine.

He and Papa didn't say much to each another during the visit, but I could tell Papa was relieved to see him.

Manman was happy beyond her wildest dreams.

Papa stayed alone in the living room while Manman and I took Moy to the kitchen to fill up a plate of food for him.

She asked him where he was staying. He said he was with a friend from school. He was going to get a job and maybe continue school while working.

"Our Moy, you are truly a man now," Manman said, clutching the hand he was not using to eat.

"When are you coming to see us again?" I asked Moy.

"Soon," he said, gently tapping me on the head, the way he always has. "You know, if I didn't see my sister for too long, I would be too sad to live."

It was just like Moy to say something like that when you were least expecting it.

"Come see us soon," I said.

"Okay," he said.

After he finished eating, Moy collected a few of his things and with a nod toward Papa, who kept his eyes on the living-room floor, he left again.

After Moy left, Manman and Papa got into an argument.

Manman asked Papa why he hadn't even said a single word to Moy.

Papa said he didn't want to talk to someone so stubborn.

"Oh yes, he is very stubborn," Manman said. "You and he are fruits from the same tree."

Friday, February 16

In homeroom, Immacula looked very agitated and worried. When I asked her what was wrong, she told me that her landlord had come over again, looking for her mother.

Immacula's mother has been working both a day and a night job since Immacula's father died.

Immacula is often late for school because she has to get her younger sisters ready as well as herself. Whenever one of Immacula's sisters is sick, Immacula must stay home. This is why she is often absent from school.

Immacula's landlord has repeatedly told Mrs. Cadet that he does not like the idea of minors being home alone so much. He is worried that without adult supervision, the girls could damage his property. Last night he threatened to throw them out or call the authorities if Mrs. Cadet does not change her situation.

Saturday, February 17

I called Moy. A girl answered the phone and then passed it to him.

He said Manman had called him earlier that day, too. They had talked about his decision to live on his own and he felt that, slowly, Manman was accepting it.

"So you're never coming back to live with us?" I asked.

"I don't know," he said.

Sunday, February 18

I wrote this letter to Papa the night I saw him cry. Today I gave it to him.

Dearest Papa,

Granpè Nozial once told me that God's tears can save us as well as drown us, but man's tears can hurt no one. With all respect to Granpè Nozial, maybe he was wrong. At least just a little. Your tears hurt me very much.

Papa, while we were apart, I cried both tears

of joy and tears of sadness. On the days before I was to come see you, I cried both.

Papa, even if you feel that we don't know each other so well anymore, please know this: We love you very much and when you were gone we missed you every day. I know this is true for you as well because you never stopped telling us in your cassettes. Perhaps it is harder for you to tell us now, without an ocean between us, but I know in my heart that it is no less true.

These are the things that you and I now share. Since I have been here in New York, I now know what it is like to live an ocean away from people you love, to not be able see them or talk to them whenever you want to. I know what it is like to not be able to share with them your reactions to the places you are seeing, the things that are happening in your life, the ideas that are in your head, the progress you are making as well as the difficulties you are facing. I have felt what it is like to watch a loved one in pain, even to blame yourself for the pain, without being able to do very much about it.

Papa, I appreciate all you have done for us and one day I hope to make you proud. I know we cannot return to the past and be the way we were in Beau Jour, but whatever family meant there and whatever it means now, I know we can be that, too.

Papa, remember when I was little and would wake up crying, thinking I had heard Galipòt at our front door? You would whisper, "Cécé, many things like Galipòt exist only in the streams of our dreams. They cannot hurt us." I want to say the same to you now, Papa. Five years of absence cannot hurt us. Besides, we are no longer a three-legged horse. We have now found our fourth and it is you.

Your daughter, Celiane

Monday, February 19

This morning, while driving me to school, Papa thanked me for my letter. His eyes were moist as he asked me what I thought he should do about Moy.

"I think you should talk to him," I said.

"I will try," he said. "For you."

Tuesday, February 20

After the threats from the landlord to throw them out or call the authorities, Immacula's mother is now sleeping at home with her daughters a few times a week. Immacula looks as though a huge burden has been lifted from her shoulders. Even though she still only wears black clothes, she smiles more often now.

Wednesday, February 21

After supper tonight, Papa had Manman call Moy to ask him to come over so the two of them could talk. I think this was the happiest telephone call Manman has made since talking to Papa from the Teleco in Léogâne.

Thursday, February 22

Moy came over and had supper with us. After a very long and heavy silence, Papa finally asked him how he was.

Moy said he was fine. He had found a job at a Laundromat and had gone back to his classes at Saint Jerome's, since he realized he needed to speak

English better in order to communicate with the customers.

Papa advised Moy to save his money, not to waste his pay.

Papa said one way Moy could save money was to come back to live with us. After all, we were going to move upstairs next month and have an extra room.

Moy thought about this for a while, then said, "I didn't like it when you told me you were going to send me back to Haiti. You leave me behind, then you send for me, then you threaten to send me back again. I am not a package. I am your son. I am a man. I had to do all the things you used to do in Beau Jour after you left. I had to step in and take your place. I am a man."

Papa said nothing for a while. He was sitting there quietly, thinking about what Moy had said.

"Okay, so you are a man," he finally spoke up. "But you will find that it's not so easy being a man."

"It has not been so easy being a boy, either," Moy said.

It was not the image I had in mind of their meeting — of handshakes and kind words — but at least before he left, Moy said he would think about living with us again, if Papa stopped treating him like a child.

Friday, February 23

I met Immacula's mother this afternoon. I stopped by Immacula's apartment to pick up a book she wanted to lend me for the weekend, when we found her mother standing outside, waiting for the school bus to bring Immacula's sisters home.

Immacula's mother is much livelier than I expected, much more jovial than Immacula, her white professional home attendant frock reminding me of Tante Rose's nursing uniform.

When Immacula introduced us, her mother leaned down for me to kiss her cheek. After I kissed her, she kept her head down so Immacula could kiss her as well. There is awkwardness between her and Immacula, like two strangers who are just getting to know one another.

Later

Franck came by to remind us that the three-bedroom apartment upstairs will be free at the end of the month. Even though we knew this was coming, we have been waiting anxiously for Franck's official announcement to begin packing.

Saturday, February 24

The people upstairs are moving. I can hear the sound of furniture being moved. Soon the apartment will be ours.

Sunday, February 25

As of tonight, the new apartment is empty. We went up to look at it this evening. It is bigger, of course, with larger windows to bring in more light. It is also a little quieter because we are two stories above the ground.

Papa immediately began to scrape the walls to prepare them for repainting. Manman and I swept the floors and scrubbed the bathroom and the kitchen, gathering every speck of dust from the old residents and throwing them away.

Monday, February 26

I received another letter from Thérèse, still with no return address. She said she might not write again because she cannot afford the postage. She has been taking stamps from her employer's bureau and she is afraid he will notice.

Thérèse was still living and working in the home of the vetiver businessman. She was able to go to school some nights, a class run by foreign missionaries.

I sensed that she wanted to make things sound much better than they were. Just as I might have exaggerated my misfortunes had I gotten another chance to write to her. Perhaps she envied me, and frankly, I felt grateful not to be in her place.

With the newly packed boxes piled up all around me, I sat in my room for a long time with Thérèse's letter pressed against my heart.

In my mind I could hear Thérèse's wonderful laugh. I wondered if she still had that deep and free laugh, which just exploded from her body like thunder and lightning from the sky. I hoped against hope that Thérèse would laugh again. And as if I were suddenly possessed by Thérèse's spirit, I raised Thérèse's letter to my throat, opened my mouth as wide as I could, pushed my head back, and laughed and laughed and laughed Thérèse's laugh. My whole body shook. My neck swiveled. My chest rattled. I waved my hands in the air, as though they were dancing.

Manman walked into the room and saw me sitting on the edge of the bed with Thérèse's letter held against my throat.

"Are you well?" she asked.

I said, "I am laughing rather than crying for Thérèse."

Tuesday, February 27

Moy brought the girl at whose apartment he has been painting to meet us. She is not a girl at all, but a woman. According to Moy, she is twenty-five years old, a whole six years older than he is. She is pretty, though not as pretty as Thérèse. She's shy and speaks in a very low voice.

Somehow, when Moy announced that he was coming back to live with us, at least until he saved enough money to rent a place of his own from Franck, she seemed a little happy.

Neither Manman or Papa appeared to like her, but they were both polite to her and didn't say anything bad about her after she left.

Wednesday, February 28

Gary's mother brought him to class to tell Mr. Marius she was sending him back to Haiti to live with his grandmother. Dressed in a suit and tie, Gary looked as uncomfortable as I had been my first day.

Mr. Marius wanted to take Gary's mother outside to talk with her, but she said she wanted us to hear what she had to say. Then she turned to the class and addressed us all as Gary lowered his head and stared down at his well-polished shoes.

"I only came for his records," she said in a tearful voice, "but I thought I would bring him to his class to say good-bye. Maybe you can all learn from this. I know he is my child and I should keep him with me, but he is always getting into trouble and he has left me no choice. I just don't know what else to do."

It was as if she was asking us all to forgive her.

Thursday, March 1

Moy has been coming over at night and going up to the new apartment with us to clean and fix things. More and more, the new apartment is starting to look like it is truly ours. Papa and Moy have painted the walls a soft eggshell white. The bathroom and kitchen are spotless.

Saturday, March 3

Today is our moving day. Moy had a bed delivered, a bed he had bought himself. Franck also came over to help us take our things upstairs.

When Papa, Manman, and I went up, we found all the walls covered with Moy's new paintings, most of which he had painted while he was gone.

I couldn't take my eyes off the paintings. They were so beautiful and so true that they left me breathless.

There it was, our voyage from Beau Jour to Brooklyn, starting with packing our things the night before leaving Beau Jour, our visit to the consulate, our plane ride and our reunion at the airport with Papa, our first walk in the snow, our first Brooklyn bus ride, the Christmas mass, the stores and houses in our Brooklyn neighborhood.

Manman walked through the apartment, staring at each canvas, as if reliving our journey, this time through Moy's eyes. Papa looked at the paintings in amazement as though he couldn't believe his own son had created them.

"When did you have time to put them up on the walls?" Papa asked Moy.

"I did it last night after the three of you went to bed," Moy said.

Franck had come over late in the night and helped Moy put up the paintings. Franck looked very proud of himself for having kept such an important secret.

"Moy's going to paint some murals in my restaurants," Franck announced. "I think that would be good, don't you, Victor?" he asked Papa.

"Very good," Papa said.

Moy asked me to be "godmother" to his series of paintings and name them.

All I could think of was the proverb, "Behind the mountains, are more mountains."

It seemed to fit. We had faced mountains of obstacles, but with help from family and friends seemed to have conquered them, at least for now.

Moy liked my suggestion of the proverb. He said that his depiction of our journey would be called "Behind the Mountains."

One day Moy's paintings will be in museums. I just

know it. People will look at these paintings and say, "This is the story of the Espérance family. This is the 'stream of their dreams.'"

Then Moy and I will write a book together. Moy will tell our story in images. And I will tell even more of our story with words.

Edwidge Danticat:
My Personal Journey

When I was two years old, my father moved to the United States from Haiti, leaving behind my mother, myself, and my younger brother, André. Papa did not want to leave us; however, he had no choice but to do so, because we were poor and he was having trouble earning enough money to take care of us, as well as our extended family — my three aunts, and two uncles — who occasionally turned to him for financial support.

At the time my father left Haiti, in 1971, the country was going through a transition from the rule of François "Papa Doc" Duvalier, who had died after having been in power for fourteen years, to his nineteen-year-old son, Jean-Claude Duvalier, who had taken his place.

Both Duvaliers had declared themselves "president for life" and imprisoned, killed, or sent into exile anyone who opposed them. Though my father was not a political exile, there were many others in our family, including my cousin Max, who had to flee Haiti at the same time because of their political views.

Two years after my father left Haiti, he sent for my mother, leaving André and me behind in the care of my uncle Joseph and his wife, Denise. André and I grew up in the Port-au-Prince neighborhood of Bel-Air, in a house filled with children whose parents had migrated to other countries — the United States, Canada, France, and the Dominican Republic — promising to send for them as soon as they were settled abroad.

It took eight years for André and me to join our parents in the United States. This was mostly because our parents needed to legalize their status — they had overstayed tourist visas — then prove to the U.S. Immigration Service that they could support us without help from U.S. government programs. In the meantime, my brothers Kelly and Karl were born in

Brooklyn, making us a family of two U.S.-born and two Haitian-born children.

When I moved to the United States at age twelve, it was a big challenge for us to become a family again. My brother Kelly, who had believed himself the first-born, suddenly found his birth order usurped and he did not like it one bit. I can still remember lengthy arguments with seven-year-old Kelly, who would try to persuade me that he was my parents' first child and that André and I were adopted from Haiti. He was so convinced of this that I began to believe it myself, reasoning that this is why our parents had allowed us to be separated from them for so long.

In spite of our poverty, which was alleviated by our parents' sending us money from New York every month, and the pressures of the younger Duvalier's dictatorship — our neighbors, parents of our friends, and teachers would sometimes disappear never to be heard from again — André and I were able to have a wonderful childhood. We would spend our summers with family members who were living in rural provinces deep in the Haitian mountains, where the wide-open skies, the beautiful streams and rivers, the music of thumping rain on tin roofs, showered us with more beauty and freedom than the city ever allowed.

My summers in the Haitian mountains were what I missed most when I moved to Brooklyn in 1981. In New York, I would look for similarities between the skyscrapers and the mountains, which had loomed over my childhood summers, and for a likeness between the winter snow and the late summer hailstorms that had seemed so magical up in the mountains.

Eventually, I adjusted to life in New York, concentrating on my junior high school studies in an English as a Second Language program, and making peace with my brother Kelly, who slowly grew accustomed to the idea that André and I were not going anywhere. However, I would never stop missing the Haitian mountain villages, which I have revisited many times as an adult, and have returned to in my imagination by writing Celiane Espérance's story in this book.

I wrote this book to explore what it might be like to move to the United States from Haiti in more recent times, especially after the turbulent period of the November 2000 Haitian presidential elections. I wanted to show, through the experiences of Celiane and Moy Espérance, how many young people who move to the United States from Haiti these days go through two kinds of migration: one from the rural areas to the Haitian capital, Port-au-Prince, then from Port-au-Prince to a major American city, in this case, New York.

Being from a family with rural origins, I have observed how many rural families, who even without advanced means of communication, such as home telephones, faxes, and e-mail, still manage to remain in close touch with their loved ones abroad through cassettes, letters, or telephone calls, scheduled for appointed times at local telephone centers in the nearest towns. That Celiane and her mother and brother have such ease communicating with Victor in Brooklyn might have been startling when I was a child, however, it is less so now. It is also not so unusual for many "country" families to have better-off "city" relatives who make their transition to eventually living abroad much easier. What might seem odd is that even though the primary language of Haiti is Creole, this diary is written in English. However I would like you to imagine that Celiane wrote these words in her native tongue and that I am merely her translator.

I would like to dedicate this book to André's and Karl's children, my three-year-old niece and nephew, Nadira and Ezekiel Danticat, who are the first second-generation Haitian-Americans (in Nadira's case Haitian-Jamaican-American) born in our family. The fact that our Haitian relatives still living in the Haitian mountains are able to look at pictures and battery-powered home video reels of them during my visits there clearly demonstrates the endless bond that exists for us between the mountains of Beauséjour, our ancestral village modeled in this book, and the skyscrapers of New York City. I hope one day to take Nadira and Ezekiel to visit these Haitian mountains with me; however, in the meantime, I will let Celiane Espérance and her "sweet little book" be their guide.

Acknowledgments

The author would like to acknowledge the following sources:

President William Jefferson Clinton's farewell address on January 18, 2001, from www.abcnews.com.
President George W. Bush's inaugural address on January 20, 2001, from www.pbs.org.
President Jean-Bertrand Aristide's inaugural address on February 7, 2001, from "BBC Summary of World Broadcasts," British Broadcasting Corporation.

I am also very grateful to the director and staff of the Isabelle Stewart Gardner Museum, in Boston, where I resided for one month during the writing of this book, and to Amy Griffin and Yves Colon for their time and effort.

Introduction to the Series

The face of America is changing. First Person Fiction, a new line of novels about today's immigrant experience, reflects this with a voice that is passionate and true. Written by authors who are immigrants themselves, these compelling stories are united by the characters' journeys to find their place as Americans.

The first two novels in the series are both told through journal entries. Through these "first person" narratives, readers will learn a lot about understanding differences, patience, loyalty and the process of adjusting to change. Both stories have strong main characters who bind their families together by helping them to adjust to a new way of life while still holding strong to their old traditions.

Discussion Points

Characters

1.   Celiane seems to be very anxious when it comes to talking to or writing to her father while she is in Haiti. What causes this anxiety? How does it lessen once she arrives in New York? Celiane describes herself as more of a country person than a city person. In what ways does she seem to change while adjusting to staying in Port-au-Prince, Haiti, and when she is in Brooklyn, New York?

2.   Manman, Celiane's mother, must take care of her children while their father is away in New York. How has the strain of their Papa being away affected her? How do Manman's sickness and injury change her? In what ways does she expect Moy to be "the man of the house" and "her little boy" at the same time?

3.   Moy has taken on the responsibilities that his father left behind and goes to school to be a tailor even though he wants to be an artist. Why do you think he remains in school to be a tailor when he loves art so much? How does Moy seem to change when he stays in the city—Port-au-Prince and Brooklyn? In what ways does Moy struggle to become a "man" in his parents' eyes?

4.   Papa, Celiane's father, moved to New York to raise money for his family to move there. How do you think his being away for so long has affected each person in the family? In what ways must he now adjust to his family being together? How does Celiane's letter to him at the end of the story change him?

5.   Tante Rose, Papa's sister, lives in Port-au-Prince and works as a nurse. In what ways does she help Celiane's family while they are in the city? Why is there such a struggle between Tante Rose and Manman?

Settings and Theme

1.   One of the proverbs in the book is "Behind the mountains are more mountains," which means that once you overcome one problem, there will always be more waiting to be solved. How does this apply to this story? In what ways does family help in overcoming such obstacles?

2.   In her journal, Celiane writes that she is afraid living in a different country and learning a different language would make her a different person. Is that true? Explain. If this were something that you had to do, how would it change you?

3.   Proverbs are used many times in this story. Celiane says a proverb "makes a picture for you and you must discover for yourself how to interpret it." How would you interpret the proverbs below and why did you interpret them the way you did?

"Little yams make a big pile."
"The empty sack does not stand."
"Sweet syrup draws ants."
"Don't look down your nose at old rags.
Remember, they fit you before."

4.   How does Grandpé Nozial's story about the man who brings the ice from the city to the mountain explain both when the family came back from Port-au-Prince and when they were leaving for New York?

5.   At the end of the story, the family comes together to live in a wonderful new apartment. Do you think this is the end of their struggles in America? Explain what other "mountains" they might find behind the mountains they have just overcome.

Websites

Haiti

Encarta Encyclopedia Article on Haiti
www.encarta.msn.com/find/concise.asp?ti=06082000

CIA — The World Fact Book
www.odci.gov/cia/publications/factbook/geos/ha/html

Haiti — www.infoplease.com/ipa/a0107612.html